by Joe R. Lansdale

Subterranean Press
2001

FIRST EDITION
June 2001

Signed, Limited Trade Edition
ISBN
1-931081-00-X

Signed, Numbered Edition
ISBN
1-931081-01-8

Subterranean Press
PO Box 190106
Burton, MI 48519

e-mail:
publisher@subterraneanpress.com

website:
www.subterraneanpress.com

ILLUSTRATIONS

To Al Sarrantonio

by Joe R. Lansdale

IF VIEWED FROM BELOW, the twelve of them appeared to be brightly colored cigars. It seemed God had clumsily dropped them from his humidor. But fall they didn't. They hung in the sky, floated on, and from time to time, as if smoked by invisible lips, they puffed steam.

If you listened carefully, and they weren't too high, you could hear their motors hum, and if it were high noon and the weather was good, you could hear the John Philip Sousa band out on the promenade, blowing and beating to knock down the heavens or raise up the devil.

INSIDE THE MAIN CABIN of the lead Zeppelin, called Old Paint due to its spotted canvas, Buffalo Bill Cody, or what was left of him, resided in his liquid-filled jar, long gray hair drifting about his head. He waited for Buntline to turn the crank and juice him up. He certainly needed it. His head felt as if it were stuffed with cotton.

Problem was, Buntline was drunk, passed out beside the table where Cody's head resided in the thick jar with the product name MASON bulged out in glass at the back of him. He was grateful that Morse had put the logo at the back of him.

The idea that he might look out at the world through the word MASON for the remaining life of his head was depressing.

Cody supposed he should be grateful that Doctor Morse and Professor Maxxon had put him here, but there were times when he felt as if he had given himself over to purgatory, or perhaps worse, a living hell.

The liquid in the jar, what Professor Maxxon called activated urine—it actually did contain a quarter pig urine, the rest was one-hundred-proof whiskey, and an amber chemical called Number 415—kept his head alive, but it couldn't keep his brain from feeling dull, sleepy even. To think right, to have the juice he needed…well, he needed Buntline to turn that goddamn crank.

Through the cabin's louvered windows, Cody could see it was high morning and the sunlight was warming up his jar. He had the horrible feeling it would heat up so much the liquid would boil and cook him. He wondered how the rest of him was doing in Morse's laboratory in Colorado. They could preserve the body all right, and they could make the heart beat, and of course they were keeping his brain alive here, but did it matter? Would head and body ever reattach?

It was too much to think about.

The lip of the brass mouth horn was fastened just inside his jaw, and when he bit down on it and talked, his voice, due to the liquid, gurgled, but he could be heard, thanks to Morse's device fastened tight in the center of his throat. He called, "Buntline, you dick cheese, get up."

Buntline did not get up.

"I'll have you tossed off this goddamn craft."

Still no Buntline.

Cody gave it up. When Buntline was truly under a drunk, which these days was most of the time, you couldn't wake him with a toot from Gabriel's horn or a kick from Satan's hoof.

Cody closed his eyes and tried to think of nothing.

But as was often the case, he thought of whiskey, women, and horseback riding. A trio in which he could no longer participate.

WILD BILL HICKOK AWOKE from Annie Oakley's beautiful ornate bed with a hard-on like a shooting iron, but Annie was gone. The bed was still warm from her and smelled of her sweetness and the sheets were wet in the center where they had made love.

Hickok suffered a tinge of guilt because he was glad Frank Butler, her former husband, was dead. Frank had been a good man, but death had certainly opened up opportunities that Hickok now dutifully enjoyed. The drawback was Annie still pined for Frank, and sometimes, after their lovemaking she would arise early to sit out on the enclosed zeppelin deck so she could feel guilty and no longer a child of God.

Hickok thought God was a fairy story, so, unlike Annie, that didn't worry him. He felt worse about Frank's memory. He thought Frank a hell of a guy, not as famous as himself, or Cody, or many of the others on board, including Annie. But like Annie, he had been a human being superior to them all.

What had made Frank good was Annie. Hickok was looking for that in himself. When he was with Annie, he felt as Frank must have, that he was worthy. That there was more to him than his speed with guns, his skill with cards, his way with whores.

Jesus, he thought. What am I thinking? I need to get the hell out of this Wild West Show and back to the real West. Away from Annie and her goodness, back to gunfights, card games and stinky whores like Calamity Jane—mean as a snake, dumb as a stone, crooked as a politician, with a face like the puckered south end of a northbound mule.

It was safer that way. You didn't get high-minded. You didn't have to stand by any morals. Calamity didn't smell good and when she left a wet spot it was something to attract insects and stick them to it, like flypaper. A woman like that you didn't attach to.

But a moment later, dressed in a long-sleeved, red wool shirt, buckskin pants and beaded boots, his long, blonde hair and mustache combed, his face washed, Hickok went looking for Annie.

ANNIE OAKLEY, LITTLE MISS SURE SHOT, twirled her dark hair with one hand, thought of Wild Bill Hickok and their love-making, and hated to admit he was far better in bed than Frank had ever been.

But a lady wasn't supposed to think about such matters. She turned her attention away from that and back to Frank, and though she missed him, knew she still loved him, his image failed to come into total focus.

It faded completely when she saw Hickok coming along the deck toward her. His tall figure, shoulder length hair, the manly nose, the cut of his hips and shoulders, made her a little queasy.

Out here on the zeppelin deck, covered by glass and wood and curtains, she thought perhaps she could think clearly. That away from his charms she could work up the courage to tell him it was over. That she would now do what she was supposed to do. Wear black till her grave and never love another man.

What courage she had summoned to do such a thing, dissolved as he sat in the deck chair beside her.

"I woke and you were gone."

"Can't go far on this craft. I'm easy to find."

He laid his hand on top of hers. "I suppose that's true."

She gently moved it away. "Not in public, Bill. I'm going back to my cabin now. To be alone. Perhaps we'll talk later."

"Certainly," Hickok said. Those clear sharp brown eyes of hers were like the wet eyes of a doe. They had the power to knock holes in his heart. He stood, watched her go away, her long black dress sweeping the hardwood decks.

STROLLING OUTSIDE ON THE PROMENADE DECK, Hickok saw Sitting Bull standing by the railing, a colorful blanket around his shoulders, his braided hair shiny with oil, decorated with a single eagle feather that fluttered in the breeze.

Hickok practically floated up to Bull, using all his woods-man's skills, but when he was within six feet of the old Sioux, Bull said, "Howdy, Wild Bill."

Wild Bill Hickok

"Howdy, Bull," Hickok said, stepping up beside him. Down below, the earth went by in black and green patches, the Pacific Ocean swelled into view, dark blue and forever.

"Been across big water many times," Bull said. "Still, fucks me over."

"Me, too," Hickok said.

"Deep. Big fish with teeth. Makes Bull's tent peg small."

"I hear that. But this beats the way we used to go. By ship. I don't know how we used to stand it. Slow. Storms. I mean, you get them up here, but you can rise above a lot of it. Course, get too high you can't breathe. Always a drawback."

Bull grunted agreement, studied Hickok. "How life, Wild Bill?"

"Good... good."

"Gettin' plenty drink?"

"Yeah."

"Good. Got tobaccy?"

"Yeah. Sure."

Hickok took out a long twist and gave it to Bull. Bull clamped down with his hard white teeth, gnawed a chunk off, began to chew. He gave Hickok back the twist.

"Gettin' pussy?"

"Oh, yeah."

"Good. Little Miss Sure Shot?"

"Gentleman don't discuss such matters."

"That why Bull ask you."

Hickok laughed.

"And if you gettin', don't tell. Little Miss Sure Shot like daughter to me. Could take your hair."

Captain Jack Crawford, the poet scout, appeared on deck. He was dressed in his beaded buckskins and wore a tan hat, the brim of which snapped in the wind. He was seldom seen without his hat. What most didn't know was that his hair, though long on the sides, was bald on top. Scalped by Cheyenne summer of '76 was the story he told, but in actuality he had been held down after a poetry reading by some miners, and with the help of Oscar Wilde, who was touring the West at the time,

Sitting Bull

they had scalped him as punishment for his poetry. Literary criticism at its most brutal.

Captain Jack stood next to Hickok, looked down at the Pacific. "Ah, the waters," he said. "Those big blue deep waters wherein, down below, the fishes hide. Where great monsters unknown lurk, and cavort…"

"Would you shut up?" Hickok said.

"Make stomach turn," Bull said. "Make tobaccy taste bad."

"Sorry," Jack said.

"Save it for those want to hear it." Hickok said. "If that's poetry, I don't want any more. All right?"

"Well, I doubt I'll be doing any recitations in Japan," Jack said. "They don't speak English."

"How bad of Japanese not speak English," Bull said. "Like dirty Indians who speak Indian words, not English."

"Custer killer," Captain Jack said.

"White eye motherfucker in wrong place at wrong time,"

Bull said. "Know Custer your friend, Hickok, but Custer still motherfucker."

"Probably right about that. Audie would poke water in a bar ditch he thought there was a fish in it, and him with that fine lookin' Libby."

"Our Savior would not want us expressing ourselves in such a manner," Captain Jack said.

"Thought white father spoke Hebrew," Bull said. "Bull speakin' English. Or almost English."

"He speaks all languages," Captain Jack said.

"Good for him," Bull said. "Him one smart God fella."

There was a moment of quiet, then Captain Jack worked the conversation back to what he wanted. "The samurai who fought with Custer. Did they make account of themselves, or did they run?"

"No arrows in yellow men's backs, not unless we sneak up from behind. They brave. Soldiers brave enough. Custer, he shit pants and shoot self."

"That is not true!" Jack said.

"True," Bull said. "Was there. You writing poetry, Bull watching white men and yellow men gettin' shot, cut, scalped. Have many swords from yellow men. Much hair from yellow and white."

"Custer had his hair," Jack said. "When they found his body he had it all. And he wasn't mutilated. So I know you're lyin'."

"Did not want hair. Ashamed of him. Custer cut it short. No hair to take. Bull hear that story how Custer not cut up. Story lie for lady Custer. He Dog cut Custer's willie off and stick in Custer's mouth. It look like it belong there. Real asshole, Custer."

"I won't hear of this," Captain Jack said, and went away.

"Good work," Hickok said.

"Bull think so."

"Custer was a friend of mine."

"Sorry."

"That's okay."

"No. Sorry Custer friend. Show Wild Bill got bad taste."

"If Yamashita had arrived on time with his planes, Terry with his zeppelins, the outcome would have been different."

"Ugh. If Bull's ass wider, deeper, could store nuts and berries for winter."

Hickok laughed. "I see your point."

"Got bottle?"

"No, but there's one in my room."

"Sound good. But must tell you. On shield, back home. Got skin off Custer's ass stretched on it. Asshole right in middle. Cleaned after bad moment on the greasy grass. You know. Custer shit self. Wild Bill friend of Custer, so thought you should know."

"You cut his ass off?"

"No. He Dog. He give to me. Said, 'Here asshole.' Have thought on that long and hard. He Dog like Bull only little better than Custer."

Hickok nodded. "Well, Custer was a friend, but you're a friend now. And frankly, I always thought that Libby Custer might have somethin' for me, and that Audie could have treated her better."

"Like Bull said, Custer friend, now Bull friend. Wild Bill's taste no better."

Hickok grinned. "Let's me and you have that drink, Bull."

Japanese biplanes buzzed them in.

The little aircraft were like hornets, flicking this way and that. They weaved in and out between zeppelins, the long white scarves of the pilots trailing like the tails of kites.

They flew near the huge cargo zeppelins where the faces and bodies of buffaloes and horses could be seen through portholes. They glided through the zeppelins' bursts of steam, were pushed back by it. They flew close enough to hear the machinery in the gear house of the zeppelins clicking and clashing like a frightened man's teeth.

On the promenade deck of Old Paint, Sousa and his band struck up a lively tune, tuba blasting, Sousa horn wailing, bass drum pounding.

Buffalo Bill Cody

Cody's head, in its jar, sat on the shoulders of a steam man, its silver body glistening in the sun. From behind, his hair floating in the preserving and charging liquid, looked like seaweed clinging to a rock.

Hickok, Annie Oakley, Capt. Jack, Bull, and Buntline, a few assorted cowboys and Indians, Cossacks, and Africans, all dressed in their finest, surrounded Cody.

The Japanese pilots flew so close to the front of Old Paint, Cody and his companions could see the slant of their eyes through their big round wind glasses. Everyone waved except the steam man. That was more trouble than it was worth.

Inside the steam man's chest, a midget named Goober worked the levers that worked the steam man. The interior of the steam man was hot and the fan that blew down from the steam man's neck only gave so much air. The grating Goober looked out of had limited vision; therefore, as the mind and reactions of the steam man, Goober had limited response.

Buntline was drunk again, but at least he was standing, his black suit looked only slightly wrinkled, his bowler hat was cocked to one side. His boots were on the wrong feet. He was trying to remember his real name before he took the name of Ned Buntline as his pen name. He smiled as he finally remembered. Ed Judson. Yeah. That was it.

He had one hand on the crank that attached to the battery in Cody's jar, and from time to time, with much effort he would crank it, giving Cody the juice. When he did, the liquid glowed, Cody's head vibrated and his hair poked at the amber fluid like jellyfish spines.

Frank Reade, the inventor of the steam man and the airships (he had improved on the German design), had donated the steam-driven man to Cody to promote his line of products. Reade had come to prominence pursuing Jesse James and his gang across the U.S. with his steam-driven team of metal horses, and now his products ruled the United States and were spreading rapidly across the world. Even if he had failed to capture James.

The steam man Cody used had been modified. The head with its conical hat through which steam had been channeled, had been removed, and the steam now puffed out a tube in the back, a tube that carried the steam above the jar and spat it high at the sky like periodic orgasmic eruptions.

Where the steam man's hat had been, Cody's jar now fastened, and on top of the jar was a great big white hat with a beaded hatband.

On the steam man's feet were specially made boots of buffalo leather, dyed red and blue, decorated with white and yellow beads. On the toes of the boots there were designs of buffaloes cavorting.

In his room, Cody had a pair that were similar, only on the toes of the boots the buffaloes were mating. He wore those when he went out with the boys.

As the zeppelins dropped, escorted by the Japanese biplanes, Japan swelled up to meet them, showed them fishing villages of stick and thatch and little running figures. Farther inland the sticks gave way to thousands of colorful soldier tents tipped with wind-snapped flags as far as the eye could see. Samurai, in bright leather, carrying long spears with banners attached and swords at their sides, lifted their helmet-covered heads to watch the zeppelins drop. From above, the Japanese in their armor appeared to be hard-shell beetles waiting for a meal to land politely into their mandibles.

As the zeppelins glided toward the long runway, bordered by soldiers, the band went silent, and Cody yelled to Goober through the talk tube. "Turn me and raise a hand."

Goober worked the controls. The steam man hissed and turned, raised a hand. Buntline, from experience, adjusted the talk tube so that it faced the crowd on the deck.

Cody boomed and gurgled. "My friends. This is an important mission. Relations with Japan over the Custer fight are strained. We are here to entertain, but we are also here as ambassadors. As role models for the others, I must ask special things of you. I need advise Mrs. Oakley not at all, but men. Stay off the liquor. They have a particularly nasty drink here called sake.

Don't touch it. Keep your Johnsons in your shorts. Pass this word along... No offense Annie."

Annie blushed.

"And men, try not to get into fights. I have dealt with the Japanese. For a time I was an ambassador to Japan. They are extremely good hand-to-hand fighters. They have a thing they call Daito Ryu Jujitsu. Boxing and brawling stand up to it poorly. They can tie you in more knots than a drunk mule skinner. Trust me on this. And in case you have not noticed, you are outnumbered. They have few guns, on the planes mostly, but they are absolutely magical with the weapons they carry. Stay in camp. You will be treated well. Abide by all the rules I have laid out, or I'm gonna be madder than the proverbial wet hen.

"So now. What do we say?"

Up went the cry: WILD WEST SHOW FOREVER.

"Hickok," Cody said sharply.

"Oh, all right," Hickok said, his face red. "Wild West Show Forever. Okay, now I've said it... I didn't hear Bull say it."

"Bull?" Cody said.

"Hey, me say thing," Bull lied.

ONCE MOORED AND DISEMBARKED, The Wild West Show—seven hundred strong, escorted by a clutch of Samurai and a robed translator who was also the Shogun's Master Physician—was amazed and delighted and a little frightened by the variety of armor and weapons, the ferocious appearance of the Japanese warriors.

Fragrances of food and body oils unfamiliar to them wafted through the air and stuffed their heads like mummy skulls packed with incense and myrrh, a musty beetle or two, a slice of raw fish.

They gravitated toward a great black tent, the peak of which was tipped with a pole and black pennant wriggling in the wind like a small ray with its tail pinned by a rock.

There was much formality. The Americans tried to bow at the right time and look pleasant. Cody, in his jar, could only grin. In his steam man arms, Cody carried a red and blue

Indian blanket wrapped around gifts from President Grant. So heavy were they, he could not have carried it with his own natural arms. The gifts were for the Shogun, Sokaku Takeda.

When the rituals were complete, Cody spoke through his tube. "From President Ulysses S. Grant to you."

Since the steam man could not bend completely over, Hickok and Bull came forward, took hold of the blanket on either side and lifted it from the steam man's arms. Sweat popped on their heads as they lowered the blanket and its burden onto a bright runner at the front of Takeda's tent.

Takeda, a small man dressed in colorful robes, his hair bound up and pinned at the back, sat, and magically, a retainer produced a camp chair. It was beneath Takeda's rear even as it appeared he would fall backwards.

Takeda spoke a few sharp words and two more retainers appeared, unrolled the blanket. Inside were eight bars of gold and eight of silver, a bright Henry rifle, two black oak-handled revolvers, their silver barrels shiny as cheap fillings in a miner's mouth. With them were two black buffalo-leather holsters pinned with silver conchos. There was also a bandoleer of ammunition.

Takeda grunted. In response to this noise, a retainer brought forth a wrapped parcel, unrolled it at the steam man's feet. Cody could not bend his neck, so the contents of the blanket were lifted and unwrapped by Hickok and Bull for his inspection.

Inside the blanket was a long sword and a short one, encased in what looked like black bone scabbards, but were in fact, highly lacquered leather.

Words were exchanged. It was determined a demonstration would be given of Grant's present by Annie Oakley.

They retired to a large patch of land next to the tent. Annie strapped on the holsters and the black-handled revolvers. She was wearing a black hat, black dress, black stockings and lace-up black shoes. She turned to Hickok and smiled.

She was so beautiful, Hickok felt his knees weaken. Then he remembered it was his job to reach into the bucket provided and toss glass balls at the sky. He snatched one, threw it high. The guns jumped from Annie's holsters. BLAM, a blast tore from one

Annie Oakley

of the revolvers and the ball burst. Hickok reached in with both hands, tossed high with his right, then high with his left, snatched up other balls and flung them rapidly, one after the other.

Annie fired first one revolver, then the other. She seemed casual, as if she were thinking about something else. But each time the balls exploded. Soon Captain Jack was helping Hickok toss. The guns snapped and the balls exploded. Annie reloaded three times, never missed.

A deck of cards was produced. Captain Jack took one from the deck, held it with the edge facing Annie. She loaded and holstered the pistols. Took a breath. The revolvers leapt from their hutches, coughed. The edge of the card was cut in two places, torn from Captain Jack's hand.

Now Bull came forward, a fat cigar in his mouth. He was puffing savagely, trying to get as much from the smoke as he could. He stood sideways, the ash on the cigar standing out a quarter inch.

Annie slowly lifted the right hand pistol, shot off the ash. She lifted the left hand pistol and shot the cigar in half. Bull pocketed the butt and stepped off the field, saying, "Machin Chilla Watanya Cicilia."

In Sioux this meant 'My daughter, Little Miss Sure Shot.'

Now Annie picked up the Henry, cocked it. "Let 'er rip," she said.

Hickok, Captain Jack, Bull, and an African Zulu king named Cetshwayo, grabbed from two buckets of glass balls and charged them at the sky. The rifle went up, moved left and right, up and down, barking at every change in direction. The balls exploded all over the sky.

Finished, Annie placed the butt of the Henry on her lace-up shoe and bowed ever so deeply. Takeda grunted. A retainer stepped forward, yelled words, the Samurai let out a roar of approval.

It was then decided Takeda would demonstrate.

He rose from his chair, which had been placed in the field, and yelled. Two armored men came charging out of the ranks, their hands lifted to strike. They struck at Takeda with extreme ferocity, but, with minimal movement, Takeda sent them flying.

They rose, came again. An arm cracked, a man screamed. Takeda struck quickly at the other. Down he went. Silent. A puff of dust from the field hung over him for a moment, thinned, disappeared.

The Wild West Show applauded politely.

The translator and Master Physician came forward then. Said to Cody, "We would like two of your men to try Master Takeda. It would be an insult not to. And it would be an insult not to try and hurt him. They must come at him hard."

Cody asked for volunteers. Hickok decided, why not, and stepped forward. With him came the tall African, Cetshwayo. Takeda nodded at them. Hickok and Cetshwayo charged. Hickok's plan was to throw a hard and powerful right, clock the little dude.

His right whistled through the air, and he knew he had Takeda, his fist was almost to the little man's temple.

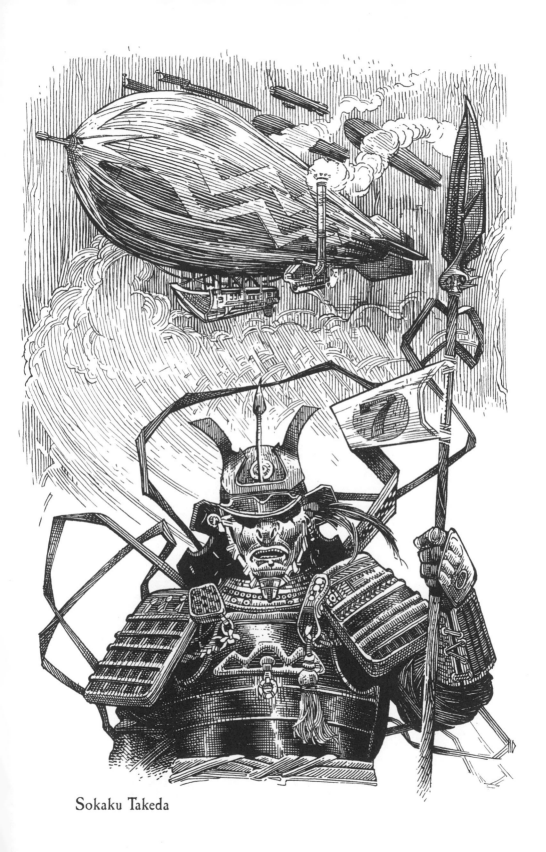

Sokaku Takeda

Then the little man wasn't there. Hickok felt pressure on his hip, then he was falling. Cetshwayo attacked by reaching for Takeda's throat with both hands. Next thing he knew, he was sailing through the air.

Jumping up, Hickok grabbed Takeda's right hand with both of his. Cetshwayo rose, struck hammer fist style at Takeda's face.

Next thing they knew, their arms were entwined and they were both on the ground, held there by Takeda's left foot.

Takeda raised his hands, his army cheered. Politely, so did The Wild West Show.

Humiliated, Hickok and Cetshwayo skulked back to their group, trying to figure on how Takeda had done it.

Takeda was handed a scabbard and sword. He poked the scabbard through his thick cloth belt. Two naked men were brought forward, they were given swords and shoved toward Takeda.

"What's happening?" Cody asked the translator through his voice horn.

"Chinese prisoners," said the translator. "They have been told that if they kill Master Takeda, they are free to go."

The Chinese, charging together, attacked the little Japanese, swords lifted high.

Takeda swayed left, then right, his sword a flash of light as it left its scabbard. One Chinaman dropped his sword, took a step, then the top half of his body fell off the bottom half. A split second later, the bottom half collapsed. While this was in progress, Takeda made a slice at the remaining swordsman.

The last Chinaman survived with only a cut across his chest. He attacked again. His sword hand went away, his wrist pumped blood. Takeda moved and let out a yell, his sword went through the man's solar plexus, out his back. With a whipping motion, the sword was freed and the man fell, as if absorbed by the earth.

"That is how the sword is used," said the translator.

"I see," Cody said.

Takeda spoke in his harsh voice. The translator bowed,

spoke to Cody. "He asks if you, or in this case, one of your retainers, would like to use the sword. We have spare Chinese."

Knowing that a trap had been laid, that Takeda was testing him, Cody said, "I would not dare make an inaccurate stroke with these metal arms. I am incapacitated. Nor would I insult Master Takeda by using a retainer. I would not want anyone else to touch such a magnificent gift as the swords given me by him, and if another sword were offered for my use, it would be an insult to his generosity."

This was duly translated. After a moment of consideration, Takeda nodded. His army cheered.

ANNIE HAD NOT MEANT TO LET IT HAPPEN AGAIN, but by nightfall she had invited Hickok into her bed. They made love for a long time, then lay together looking at the ceiling, bathed in soft lantern light.

"Takeda murdered those men," Annie said.

"Yes he did," Hickok said.

"Savages."

"Not too unlike what we did to Bull's people."

"Not like that. Surely, it wasn't like that."

"I guess you never heard of Sand Creek?"

"I don't want to."

"Neither do most white people. Especially since innocent Cheyenne were slaughtered there for the amusement of white Colorado Volunteers. Women and children were scalped. Tobacco bags were made from parts of their skins, their private parts. And the Little Big Horn. My friend Audie was killed there, and made into a hero, but he was a fool. The Sioux and the Cheyenne were merely protecting themselves, and we call it a massacre."

Annie rose up, put her back against the oak headboard. Though normally modest, now mad, she allowed the sheet to slip away, revealing her breasts. In the lantern light the nipples stuck out like the tips of .44 caliber slugs, the rings around her nipples were dark as burnt powder.

In spite of her anger, or perhaps because of it, Hickok felt aroused again.

"Are you saying I don't care about what was done to Indians? You know better. Bull is an Indian and I love him dearly."

"I'm saying, you're human. Like me. We don't see what's in our own country as bad, anymore than these folks do. Or by the time we do, it's too late."

Annie relaxed. "You've changed, Bill. I never knew you to feel this way."

"The Wild West Show, which I don't care for, I might add, changed me. I don't like all these plays and speechifying, but when you spend enough time with people with different skin you start thinking of them differently."

"You're a real pain, Bill. Frank never disagreed with me."

"I'm not Frank."

"You certainly aren't."

"Is that good or bad?"

"I'm beginning to think it's good." Annie took hold of one of her breasts, arched her back, and in a voice Hickok had never heard before, said, "Baby, you want to nurse?"

"Oh. You betcha."

INSIDE THE BLACK AND YELLOW TENT of the Master Physician, Sokaku Takeda, thirty-third grandmaster of Daito Ryu Aikijujutsu, sponsor of the diplomatic invitation to The Wild West Show, Shogun, soon to be ruler of Japan, watched as two soldiers held the monster's lashed down left leg firm.

When the soldiers had it held tight, the Master Physician sawed off the remaining piece of the monster's left foot, not bothering to cauterize the wound. There was no point. There was no blood in the creature. It was, however, decided it would be best to screw a block of wood to the ankle so they could walk the thing back to its cell and not have to lift it from the carving table and carry it.

Though the monster had no blood, no beating heart, it lived. Its oily black eyes rolled in its greenish face, it shook its head, causing its long, greasy, black hair to thrash back and forth like a veil in a crosswind.

Alive or not, as the soldiers put the block to its nubbed ankle and pushed in the screw with a driver, it bellowed like a bull, began to curse Takeda and all his descendants in guttural English.

The chunk taken from the monster's foot was placed on a small wood-block table. The Master Physician cut, sliced, and diced the piece of dead flesh into a dozen pieces, placed the particles in a little bronze bowl, poured scented oil on it and set it on fire.

The flame leapt green, yellow, subsided. The physician ground the remains into a fine black powder with a pestle. He used a thick piece of cotton to pick up the bowl and pour the smoking ashes into a bowl of water. This in turn was run through a white cloth, leaving black residue on the surface. The residue was placed in a rice paper envelope, folded, sealed with wax, given to Takeda, the Master Physician bowing low in the process.

"How long will he last?" Takeda asked.

"He feels pain, but his body is not really harmed like that of a living man. Master Takeda, he will last a long time. I believe he will be alive when only the head is left. Doctor Frankenstein developed a process that causes his brain to live and make the body function. There is blood, but it has nothing to do with life. It congeals more than it runs."

"Does he eat?"

"He must eat."

"Does he defecate?"

"Like a water buffalo, sire. He has all the urges of man, but he is a false man. He does not bleed true blood, just the congealed goo. He does not sweat."

Takeda turned to where the naked monster lay lashed to the table. The creature was tall, and in a way, attractive. But his legs didn't match. You could see scars where the legs had been fastened with thread and bolts to his hips, same for the knees. His shoulders, elbows, wrists and ankles showed the same sorts of scars. His genitals were massive; testicles like grapefruits, a penis like a dagger scabbard.

The face was the thing, however. It was greenish, the eyes gray and watery. There seemed to be too much bone for the available skin; it didn't fit right. The lips were black as charcoal, the teeth horse-like and of poor quality.

"You are strange," said Takeda in Japanese.

The monster, having been a captive now for six months, a piece of him whittled away daily, could understand enough Japanese to know what was said. He replied in English.

"You eat of my flesh to make yourself hard, and you say I am strange. Yours is a life of oddness and ritual, the bizarreness of the living. Like my former creator, Victor Frankenstein, long lost now among the ice floes of the Arctic in a skating accident, I have only simple dark words for you. Eat shit, little man."

Of course Takeda did not speak English, nor did the soldiers. The Master Physician did, but he lied to Takeda, told him the monster was asking to be freed.

"Only when the last of you is gone," Takeda said. "Think of it this way. What residue of you my body does not absorb is passed through my bowels. That is how you will escape. As turds."

Takeda exited the tent with his little envelope of burned, ground flesh.

SOKAKU TAKEDA HEADED BACK TO HIS TENT where naked women waited. He had learned from the Master of Apothecary that there was something in the flesh of the creature that, when prepared properly, served as an aphrodisiac. It gave him the energy to spread his seed among his concubines. For if there was one thing he wanted, it was a male heir. He already had several daughters. So many he had sold some of them to Chinese merchants and one American who wanted a pet. What he needed was a son. Someone to teach Daito Ryu to. Someone to hand down his kingdom to, for it was just a matter of time before the old ruler collapsed under the weight of his army and ambition. And, in the meantime, this son business, well, it was fun trying to make the little guy.

Ned Buntline

WHEN TAKEDA HAD DEPARTED and the soldiers had taken the monster away, the Master Physician seated himself in a corner and opened a drawer hidden in his desk. From it he took a little machine with lettered keys and extensor antennae.

When he had the antenna pulled to its full length, he began to tap out a message on the keys.

Inside Cody's cabin, on the dresser, next to the jar that held his head, a duplicate machine began to snap. Cody opened his eyes, yelled through the voice tube for Buntline.

Buntline, pinning a chair to the floor with his butt, rose, staggered to the machine, grabbed up a pad and pencil, wrote out the message.

He read it to Cody.

Cody spoke to Buntline. A moment later, Buntline was tapping the keys.

NEXT MORNING WAS FULL OF POMP AND CIRCUMSTANCE. The Wild West Show in all its colorful glory, paraded between the Japanese tents and soldiers, Sousa and his band playing *Gerry Owen*.

There were livestock, stagecoaches, covered wagons, buckboards, all manner of riders and rigs, and, of course, the beautiful Annie Oakley waving from the back of a big white horse. Last, but certainly not least, came the head of Buffalo Bill Cody. Cody rode in a buckboard, on the lap of Buntline, who was not overly drunk this day. From time to time, Buntline would raise the jar containing Cody's head, lift it to the left, then to the right.

There were cheers, but they were more polite than inspired.

"Tough bunch," Buntline said.

"They only cheer when they're supposed to," Cody said. "Takeda runs this show."

"Not The Wild West Show, he doesn't," Buntline said, hoping Cody would remember this later and offer him a bottle from his good stock of special whiskey.

"Not yet," Cody said. "But he makes me nervous. This is the first show where cutting up a man was part of our arrival celebration. Cast and crew, Annie I know, were more than a little upset. Could affect their performance, and if it's one place we want to look good, it's here."

"Would you like a little crank?" Buntline asked.

"Not just yet," Cody said.

They rode the rest of the way in silence.

Parade over, The Wild West Show was quickly constructed. The show was a traveling community with carpenters, painters, blacksmiths, tailors, doctors, barbers, stock handlers, gunsmiths, boot and shoemakers, washers and ironers, cooks and prostitutes. Everyone had a job and did it with speed and precision.

Tents leapt from the ground, poked summit poles at the sky. Corrals snapped together and the stock was thunderously yee-hawed inside. Water tanks were filled, food tents were packed with supplies and tables.

Inside Cody's tent, the tip of which was peaked with the American flag, the steam man was in the process of being painted so he would appear to be wearing a buckskin jacket, cream trousers, and a crimson shirt dotted with blue and white prairie flowers. Over this, colored beads and soft leather tassels would be glued in the appropriate places. The jar containing Cody's head would be attached, different boots would be placed on the steam man's feet; they would be dark chocolate colored knee-highs with bright red suns on the toes as a goodwill gesture to the Japanese empire. Last but not least, a wide-brimmed, white hat with a beaded hat band would be pushed down over the top of the jar.

Goober, the midget, would be inside the steam man, out of sight, wearing nothing more than a g-string, fighting the heat, fighting the gears, the little steam-powered fan in the neck of the machine blowing hot air down his back.

When the show was over, Goober would be hosed down, laid out and fanned by four assistants. Cooled, Goober would be hosed again, dried, fed, then allowed to sleep.

The steam man would be cleaned with turpentine and soap, dried, ready to be repainted. Cody had discovered long ago that, with the exception of the boots and hat, dressing the steam man made him look too bulky. This method kept him streamlined. From a distance, even relatively close, no one could tell it was paint and showmanship instead of clothes.

That night, electric lights powered by the show's steam generators, as well as strings of bright Japanese lanterns strung on high poles, illuminated the scene. Around the field The Wild West Show had thrown up rows of bleachers as well as concession stands where taffy, popped corn, parched peanuts, cotton candy, and American beer could be bought.

Once the show started, the crowd, though not particularly loud or rowdy to begin with, went stone silent. Soon Annie was at work doing her trick shooting. Her husband and helper, Frank, was gone, but now she had Hickok to assist her, keeping her guns loaded, her props in place. She started by having Hickok release four clay pigeons simultaneously.

The moment they were sprung, she ran toward the bench where her guns lay, leapt over it, grabbed up a Winchester, and burst all the launched targets before they could touch the ground.

A roar went up from the crowd. They were not only amazed at her marksmanship, but at the rifle itself, as Japanese exposure to fine firearms was limited.

More clay pigeons were released and burst. A playing card was cut. Strings dangling from a hat were picked off one by one at a great distance. One impossible shot after another was made.

Finished, Annie raised her arms, slowly bowed. The normally sedate Japanese warriors broke into a cheer. Takeda, sitting on a stool at the front of his tent, stood and bowed to Annie.

A rider burst out of nowhere on a black horse, galloping toward Annie at full speed. He extended a hand. Annie grabbed, swung onto the back of the saddle, and away the horse thundered. Again the crowd cheered.

Shortly thereafter came a horde of cowboys, doing tricks on horseback, roping and shooting at targets. Cattle were released. The cowboys roped, threw, and tied them.

Stagecoaches thundered around the makeshift arena, pursued by Indians who leapt onto them from their horses. Mock fist and knife fights took place, cartridge blanks snapped and exploded.

Scouts of the Prairie, a play, was performed in the center of the arena with Hickok, Captain Jack and Cody. It was translated by the interpreter who called out the words in Japanese over a megaphone. His words were in turn passed throughout the crowd by other Japanese armed with megaphones.

It was not an entirely successful moment. The play was bad to begin with. There was the language barrier. And every time Cody moved there was hesitation as Goober responded to orders tossed down the pipe. The interpreter sometimes mistook these words as part of the play, presented Cody's commands, curse words and oaths to the perplexity of the crowd.

The next act bought the crowd's enthusiasm back. A small log cabin was fastened together quickly in the center of the arena. Thatch was tossed over the top to serve as a roof.

A clothesline was hastily erected, a wash pot and scrub board were placed nearby. A woman and her children, a boy and a girl, appeared. The woman pretended to do her wash in the wash pot. She hung a couple of items on the line.

Suddenly, out of nowhere came a horde of Indians. The mother and her children retreated inside the cabin. A window was opened. The mother poked a rifle out, shot at the Indians as they circled the cabin on their horses, hooting and hollering and firing off blanks.

Then a torch was thrown on the cabin's roof. The prepared straw and kerosene sprang to life. It looked as if the woman and her children would be burned alive. An Indian leapt off his horse, grabbed at the cabin door.

The lock snapped free, the Indian rushed in. The woman and her children were pulled into the yard. The roof of the cabin blazed. An Indian painted in heavy war paint pulled a tomahawk from his belt, and just as he was about to cut down on the woman, there was a bugle blast.

Twenty men in cavalry uniforms, Cody at their head, his steam man torso mounted on one of Frank Reade's shiny steam horses, rode into view. The steam horse hissed clots of vapor, its metal hooves stamped the ground. The Indians released their captives, bounded onto their mounts and fled, the cavalry and Buffalo Bill Cody in hot pursuit.

Saved, the women and children ran out of the arena. A steam-powered fire engine chugged up. The cabin's roof was doused with water from a large hose. Men dismantled the cabin, and away it went, providing room for the next feature.

OFF-STAGE CODY WAS LIFTED FROM HIS HORSE with a crane. When the steam man was on the ground and the cowboys had unfastened the harness, Buntline appeared with a screwdriver, and removed Cody's head from the torso.

While he was doing this, Goober opened the door in the steam man's ass and slid out backwards like a plump white turd. He got up with dirt sticking to his sweaty body, and without a word, wandered off to be hosed.

Annie and Hickok were nearby, cleaning the weapons Annie had used in her act. A cowboy wandered up. He said to Cody's head, "You heard them yellow men got them a fella they're cuttin' up?"

"What?" Cody asked.

"A fella. They're cuttin' on him. And he ain't no Chinese or Jap neither. I think he's a white feller."

"Say he is," Cody said. "Where did you hear that?"

"That boy, Tom Mix."

"The elephant handler," Cody said. "Well, it's most likely a damn lie. But I'll look into it." Then to Buntline: "Get my head inside the tent. These electric lights are making me hot. I feel hungry, too."

The cowboy rode away.

"You don't eat," Buntline said.

"I know that, you idiot. How in the world did you ever write my adventures."

"Hell, I just do what you do. I make them up."

Buntline picked up Cody and started for their tent.

Annie said to Hickok, "They're cutting up a man? You mean like those poor Chinese?"

"I don't know," Hickok said. "It wouldn't surprise me to discover they're cutting on someone most of the time. But I won't lie to you. My curiosity is getting the better of me."

Hickok lay the Winchester he was cleaning on the bench, wiped the gun oil from his hands, headed for Cody's tent, Annie walking alongside.

Hickok threw back the flap on Cody's tent, peeked inside. Cody's jar had been placed on a crate. The lid of the jar had been removed, and Buntline, with a long straw, was poking through the liquid into a hole in the top of Cody's head.

"Oh, yeah. That feels good. I feel like I'm eating something."

"What's it taste like?" Buntline asked.

"Anything and everything," Cody said, "but I'm going to think it's a big buffalo steak with a burnt potato. And beer. Plenty of beer."

"I don't mean to interrupt you at mealtime," Hickok said. "But we overheard that cowboy out there, and since it's none of our business, we thought we'd ask what that was all about... a man being cut up and all."

"Come in," Cody said. "That Annie with you? Why sure, come in, darlin'. Good show. You've never been better. *Scouts of the Prairie* certainly went over like a lead balloon, didn't it Wild Bill?"

"Far as I'm concerned, it always does."

"What exactly is it you and Ned are doing?" Annie asked Cody. "Or should I ask?"

"I'm eating. Sort of."

"Doctor Chuck Darwin came up with it after the accident," Buntline said. "Him and Morse. Darwin discovered that if you stimulated certain parts of the brain in rats, they thought they had eaten. You could do this until the little buggers died of starvation. But they'd think they were full. Having worked on rats, Darwin thought it would work on Buffalo Bill, his ownself. And it does."

"Won't you starve to death too?" Annie asked.

"Not in this fluid," Cody said. "And Morse is taking care of the body. Someday, we'll reconnect them. And I'll be slimmer to boot. Morse told me last time we talked that he'd allowed the body to shed a few pounds."

"About this man being cut," Hickok said. "Know about it?"

Cody was silent for a moment. He said, "Ned. Put the lid on the jar, then I want you and Annie to listen, Bill. I know who it is being cut up. It's why we're here."

"I thought we were here for a Wild West Show," Annie said.

"I thought we were here on a kind of diplomatic mission," Hickok said. .

"Yes and yes...and no," Cody said. "President Grant thought after the disaster at the Little Big Horn, all those Japanese warriors being slain under Custer's fool command...well, we needed some diplomatic work. But there's more."

"I don't keep up with politics," Annie said. "Enlighten me."

"Ever since the Japanese discovered America's West Coast, and the Europeans discovered the East Coast, there's been tension. In the last few years our expansion has outdone that of the Japanese, and both nations have crushed the Indian in the middle. We've even worked together at doing it. Now, well, frankly, after the Civil War and the founding of Texas as a Negro state, it seems the U.S. is interested in removing the Japanese from our continent. The recent annexing of Canada as the twentieth state, and with all the western territory we now own, Grant would like to see us own all the land to the western coast.

"But the Japanese won't sell. Takeda, he's the most powerful ruler in Japan. With our help, or without it, he will eventually rule all of Japan. But with our help it would be easier. That's why I presented him with firearms. To give him some idea of their usefulness. Japanese firearms are so primitive."

"He's going to use a rifle and a couple of handguns to rule Japan?" Annie said.

"If he likes what he sees," Cody said, "President Grant will supply more. And the guns will, obviously, make his conquest easier.

"In fact, on this trip, I have secretly had a case of Winchesters presented to him, along with a case of ammunition. For our assistance, he is supposed to sign a pact with our country offering us the West Coast. Only, there have been some recent flies in the ointment."

"Such as?" Hickok asked.

"Such as Mexico. They're still mad about San Jacinto. For the last thirty years or so they've been looking to stick it to us. They're offering the Japanese the same guns, but they're not asking them to give up land. They merely want them as allies."

"Didn't our country just give Mexico guns they didn't have a couple years back?" Hickok asked. "Some kind of diplomatic gift?"

"We did," Cody said. "Now they make their own. And good quality, too."

"So why are we here wasting our time?" Hickok said. "If they can get the guns from Mexico without having to give up land, then we're kind of done in, aren't we?"

"We didn't know that when we set out. I received the information by telewire this morning. The Verne satellite beamed it in."

"We seem to have lost our fella that was gettin' cut up," Hickok said.

"We'll come back to that," Cody said. "I came here as a diplomat for our president, but I had an ulterior motive."

Cody paused as a cheer resounded in the arena.

That would be the stagecoach trick, thought Cody. It made him feel good to hear that cheer. It always did.

Hickok offered Annie a camp stool, folded out one for himself, sat down. Cody suggested they break open a bottle, and Buntline was quick to grab it from Cody's private stash. Whiskey was poured for Hickok and Buntline. Annie declined. Cody, of course, was forced to pass. He said, "Drink a bit for me."

"You betcha," Buntline said.

"Give me a crank, Ned. Give me two."

Buntline complied. Cody's hair stood on end and the jar glowed. When the moment passed, Cody's hair collapsed in the fluid to float. And Cody began to talk.

"ONCE UP A TIME I HAD A BODY WITH THIS HEAD. Pretty damn good body, I might add. I've told many tales about how I ended up this way, but, as you might suspect, they are all lies, some of them concocted by my friend Buntline here.

"My head was not cut off with a tomahawk, as has been reported, nor did I have an accident learning to fly an airplane or drive one of those horseless carriages. Nor was I in an incident with a herd of swine. That's one I didn't make up, I'm quick to admit. That was one of Buntline's. Turn the crank, will you, Ned."

Ned took hold of the crank and went to work.

"That's better. It all happened back at my place, The Welcome Wigwam on the North Platte. Christmas of two years ago. It was a great night at home. It was cold as a castrated pig's nuts in a tin basin, and it was snowing. Louisa and I had guests. Sam Morse and his wife. Their friends Professor Maxxon, his lab assistant, B. Harper, and his lovely wife Ginny. Also present was the beautiful young stage performer, Lily

Langtry. They were spending the night with us. The Morses and Maxxons in the guest house, all others in the main house. There had been much playing of the piano and singing aloud around the Christmas tree. The usual holiday frivolities.

"Truth was, Morse, Maxxon and Harper were there to do scientific work in my outbuildings. They were trying to bring a cadaver back to life. A horrible thing, I assure you, but fascinating nonetheless, and I was anxious to have them there because they were such good company, and because Miss Langtry was a dear friend of Sam Morse's. A lovely woman, clothed or unclothed. Wonderful as a spring morning, only a lot more fun.

"The good news was my wife, Louisa, went to bed early. And I went to bed not much later. With Miss Langtry. The bad news is my wife, normally a sound sleeper, slept less soundly this night, and Miss Langtry, a vocal nightingale under any circumstance, hit a high note during our visitation. It awoke Louisa. She discovered us together, took the fire axe from the dining hall and struck me from behind.

"It wasn't a killing blow, but it nearly severed my head from my shoulders. Once Louisa realized what she had done, she let out a scream that awoke Morse and the others. Miss Langtry began to scream as well.

"Morse immediately set about stopping the flow of blood, and with the aid of Harper and Maxxon, got me out to the lab they had made in one of my outbuildings. They immediately placed me in the bathtub there and packed it with snow. I don't remember feeling cold, or feeling much of anything. I vaguely remember the tub was where they cut up dead bodies for use in their research, and now I was in it. But I didn't give that much thought. I was sailing away, folks, that's what I was doing. The Happy Hunting grounds had done thrown me up a teepee.

"Well sir, Maxxon and Morse struck upon a bold plan. They had had no success in reviving a corpse, but perhaps their knowledge could save me. Morse contrived the battery jar, the fluid was a creation of Maxxon's. He had been using the fluid for some time as a preservative for body parts.

"They had been working on the theory that if you charged Morse's electrical energy into Maxxon's chemicals, it would not only act as a method of preserving, but would actually cause the nerves in severed limbs, and perhaps even brain cells, to continue to function.

"Since I didn't have a lot of options, they decided to operate. My head was completely removed, placed in this jar you now see, and an electric current was applied.

"Obviously, it worked. Later, the battery, the cranker, and the voice horn were added. Then of course Frank Reade provided the steam man's body and Doctor Charles Darwin has made a few suggestions. But the bottom line is yet to come. And that is Victor Frankenstein."

"Frankenstein?" Annie said. "I thought that was just a story. This all sounds like a story. One of your stories."

"This one's true, Annie. And Frankenstein, he's real. And so is his monster. Morse and Maxxon were much aware of Frankenstein's work, but had been unable to duplicate it.

"Maxxon had tried to produce a man out of chemicals, what he called the very stew of life, but had failed. As you might suspect, he was not vocal about his results, for obvious reasons. He had failed, and the fact that he had tried was enough for some authorities and citizens to rise up in arms and maybe lynch him. The very idea of it was aberrant to many."

"It's aberrant to me," Annie said.

"I just recently learned that word," Cody said. "And I've been wanting to work it into conversation. How did I do?"

"Good enough," Hickok said.

"So, it's aberrant to you, Annie," Cody said. "But think about it. Without it, I wouldn't be here."

"But you weren't created," Annie said. "You were saved. That's not the same as bringing back the dead, or creating a human being out of electricity and chemicals."

"True," Cody said. "That kind of business upsets the Christians, and I don't think it does the Moslems any good either. But it can be done. Frankenstein managed to cobble dead bodies into a man, and with a charge of lightning, brought it to life.

36

"Morse and Maxxon teamed up, decided to try and approach Doctor Frankenstein, and Doctor Momo, another scientist working on the problem, to see if collectively they could find an answer. Something more successful than a living dead man. They felt with Maxxon's knowledge of chemicals, Morse's of electricity, Frankenstein's knowledge of anatomy, and Momo's understanding of surgery, they would be able to fill in the blanks for one another.

"How would this help you?" Bill said.

"In the process of learning how to create a human being, they felt assured they could, with Frankenstein's help, refasten my body to its head. Use me as a kind of lab rat. An experiment in preparation for the greater experiment.

"However, Momo was eliminated immediately. He had left England some time before and had not been heard from since. It was rumored he had lost his marbles.

"Then it was learned that Frankenstein had gone to the Arctic in search of his creation. It was his intent to kill it. Story isn't clear, but it's said the Doctor was lost in the frozen waste, perhaps killed by his creation. Certainly the monster killed Frankenstein's wife, so the creature was capable of it."

"How horrible," Annie said. "That's the kind of result you can expect, tampering with nature."

"Perhaps," Cody said. "But the creature turned up in Russia, was captured, sold to Takeda. This we knew. Takeda bought him with the express purpose of making aphrodisiacs by cutting off pieces of him and turning them into a powder. This was on the advice of his Master Physician, who has ulterior motives. Like finding out what makes this creature live."

"How do you know that?" Bill asked.

"Because the Master Physician is an agent for the United States. He has scientific interests that are smothered by Takeda's war interests. He's been turning information over to our country with the understanding that he may come to the U.S. to live, and there have the opportunity to expand his knowledge and interest in medicine.

"The Master Physician offered the creature to our country along with the information he was providing. Our country was not all that interested in the thing, but I was. And so were the good doctors who saved me.

"So, when there was an opportunity to take The Wild West Show here on a diplomatic mission, I jumped at the chance. I thought I might kill two birds with one large rock. I'd make a good deal for our country with Takeda, then maybe make a personal deal for the monster, take him home for Morse and Maxxon to look over and study. The first part of the plan is shot. I know that now. And I doubt that helps the second part of the plan. So, what we're going to do is something different."

"How different?" Hickok asked.

"We're gonna steal the old boy and hustle him home to Welcome Wigwam where the boys, wives and assistants, and of course the smug Louisa, wait to do their work. They on the monster, Louisa on me. Her tongue is as sharp as any scalpel."

"How did it work out with Miss Langtry and your wife?" Annie asked.

"Louisa apologized, but I got to tell you, an apology for something like that, it just doesn't have the impact you'd hope for. I forgave her, but I didn't forget. I'm thinking of divorce.

"As for Miss Langtry, she was disappointed in the whole state of affairs, especially since we failed to finish our mission of that night, but pledged silence. She went home on the next train. I suspect she's doing now what she's always done. Performing in stage shows."

"With donkeys and her tied to a barrel," Annie said.

"What was that?" Cody said. "Speak up."

"I said, you can't really blame your wife. You're not exactly the most faithful husband in the world."

"Well, dear, not everyone can be like your Frank, God bless his soul. I was at fault, no doubt, for I love a skirt, or rather, and pardon my boldness, what is under it. But chopping off my goddamn head. Now that's severe."

"Not in my book," Annie said.

"I'm not trying to force anyone to get involved with my plight," Cody said. "But if I can convince just a few, for it is a mission better accomplished by a few, to help me, then I have a chance to live a normal life. The creature will be spared a slow death, brought home for honest scientific study."

"Won't he be cut up there?" Annie said.

"Possibly," Cody said.

"Then what's better about his situation?" Annie asked.

"Oh, hell," Cody said. "I admit I'm more worried about my situation. Look at it this way. He's dead already, so what's to lose?"

"Nothing says he'll certainly be dissected?" Hickok said. "Am I right?"

"Right," Cody said.

"Then at least he's better off for a while, and maybe forever," Hickok said.

"I don't feel right about it," Annie said.

"Count me in," Hickok said.

"Ned?" Cody asked.

"I get whiskey out of this deal?"

"You do."

"I'm in."

"Annie, darling. What about you?"

"I don't like it," Annie said. "But since the Japanese are double-crossing our government, and it gives the monster some chance at freedom, why not?"

"Good," Cody said. "It's wonderful to have you. There are a few others I'm going to ask for assistance. But only a few. A small group is best. And we'll only need a skeleton crew to operate my personal zeppelin. We'll send everyone else home, then…well, let's just hope the Japanese don't read Homer and the Master Physician is as trustworthy a spy as he seems. He did, after all, study at Harvard. Ned. The time."

Ned removed his pocket watch from his pants pocket, opened it, told Cody the time.

"Two hours from now, the Master Physician will be ready to receive a message. Ned, this is what I want you to tell him…"

WHEN THE SHOW CAME TO AN END THAT NIGHT, and ceremonies were observed, Cody set a crew of men to work. By morning the mules were pulling a large wheeled platform into the arena, near the edge, next to the great tent of the Master Physician.

The platform was thirty feet long, twenty feet wide and five feet deep. On it sat a Conestoga wagon fashioned from the lumber of prefab animal pens and leather. It had been worked on carefully by Cody's craftsmen: carpenters, tailors, etc. It was a beautiful thing. The leather covering of the Conestoga—mocking what should actually have been canvas—was brightly painted with trees, buffalo and a rising sun. Inside the Conestoga were a number of gifts. Indian blankets, beaver hats, jerked meat, jarred jellies, and a fairly life-like female sex doll fashioned from leather, paint, and human hair. The doll had been pumped full of air, and had the proper anatomical adjustments.

Almost instantly after the delivery of the Conestoga, The Wild West show folded and loaded. The zeppelins rose, their steam driven motors kicked in, and they sailed west, leaving their gift behind.

The delivery of the wagon had not gone unnoticed by the Japanese. The departure of the American fleet had been rude and unceremonious, but at least they had left a box of treasures. Takeda surveyed them, had the wagon searched for trap doors and the like, found none. He gave a few of the gifts to select soldiers, placed the wagon under guard, then retired to his tent with the leather blow-up doll and the intention of testing its function.

Deep in the night, the wind came down out of the north and brought dampness with it, spread it over the great camp of Takeda, and over the unlucky guards protecting the gift from The Wild West Show. The air turned chilly, and so did the soldiers.

The Master Physician, feigning insomnia, came from his tent smiling, carrying a gourd full of sake. He offered some to each of the guards in little wooden cups he carried in a knotted rope bag coated in wax. Shortly after swallowing the liquor, all of the guards collapsed into a deep sleep. Later, early

The Monster

morning, they would be awakened by their skin being removed slowly from their bodies with a sharp piece of bamboo. Their reward for failure.

When the guards collapsed, the Master Physician gave the side of the wagon's platform a hard kick. Hesitated. Kicked again. Then kicked twice. He immediately disappeared inside his tent.

The sides of the platform on which the wagon rested opened, and a very hot and uncomfortable group of men, and Annie, all dressed in black, their faces smeared with ash, (except Cetshwayo, whose skin was already black as the night sky) slid out into the darkness and rain, and slipped into the nearby tent of the Master Physician.

Inside there was only one lantern burning. But Hickok, Cetshwayo, Annie, Bull, and Captain Jack, had enough light to see the Master Physician and a man seated on the ground, dressed in a blue and white kimono. He had a leather mask over the lower half of his face, his feet—one foot actually and a block of wood—were bound in front of him, his hands behind his back. For insurance, he had been wrapped in strong silk cord.

"We must hurry," said the Master Physician, "otherwise, we are up what you Americans call shit creek."

"This is the creature?" Annie asked.

"It is," said the Physician.

"Why, he looks like any other man. Except for that block of wood on his foot."

"And the green skin," Hickok said.

"Him look sick," said Bull.

"What happened to his foot?" Annie asked.

"It would take too long to explain," said the Master Physician. "And remember, looks can be deceiving. He is not like any other man. Stand closer, away from the direct glow of the lantern. His skin is strange. Touch him. It's like touching a corpse. He is a corpse."

"Important thing is to grab the rascal, and haul ass before Takeda figures out what's going on," Hickok said. "Send the message, physician."

The Master Physician opened the secret panel in his desk, brought out the machine, raised the antenna, began to tap out a message.

Hickok cut the silk rope around the creature's legs and body. He and Bull raised the creature to his feet. Hickok was amazed at the size of the man. He must have been over seven feet tall, with shoulders considerably broader than his own. Hickok said, "You can understand English can't you?"

The creature nodded.

"Good. Now I know you can't talk with that gag on, but you can listen good. I got a .44 here, and if you mess with me I'm gonna blow what brains you got—whoever they originally belonged to—all over this place. Savvy? Nod your head if you do."

The creature nodded.

"You would have to splatter his brains for him to really be affected," the Master Physician said. "Remember. He is not a man."

Hickok ignored the physician, spoke firmly to the creature.

"Remember, I'm here to save your patchwork ass."

The creature nodded.

"I'm gonna have my friend Bull here cut your legs loose when the zeppelin shows up, and you're gonna go with us. Can you stump on that block of wood all right?"

The creature nodded.

The Master Physician stood at the front of the tent, near the flap, looking out at the night and the rain, which had begun to hammer the camp. "A light," he said.

He was referring to a light from the zeppelin. As planned, all other lights on the craft had been turned off, but the fore-deck beam blinked once through the night and the rain, went black.

A moment later, three rope ladders coated with a glowing chemical, were dropped from the zeppelin. The Master Physician was the first one out of the tent, the others followed. Hickok, Bull and the creature brought up the rear. The creature with his wood block foot was no runner. He stumped and sloshed mud.

44

As they grabbed the ladders, began to climb, a cry went up in the camp. They had been spotted. From the ground, at first glance, it appeared they were ascending glowing magic ladders hung in the air; it was only with a bit of eye strain that one could see the shape of the zeppelin through the night and the rain.

The zeppelin's foredeck and open promenade lay under the great interconnecting cells of helium, the ladders were fastened to the railing of the promenade. Annie was the first on board, then the Master Physician, followed closely by Cetshwayo, and Captain Jack.

On the last ladder was Bull, the creature, and Hickok bringing up the rear. The creature, heavy and slow, was climbing with difficulty. An arrow whistled by Hickok's head. He turned and looked.

Down below fire burned in pots, hissed in the rain, coughed white smoke. The flames, fueled by some remarkable propellant, leapt orange and yellow through the smoke. From high above, they were like redheads and blondes, hopping on the balls of their feet, bouncing their heads above a morning mist.

Hickok hung to the rope with one hand, jerked his revolver loose with the other, fired at the pots, bursting four of them, smashing the fires in all directions.

More pots were lit, and more arrows were launched. One went through Hickok's trousers, hung there, just below the knee. Hickok slipped his revolver back in the sash at his waist and tried to climb faster, but all he could see was the monster's legs, the block of wood, and under the kimono. Hickok was disgusted to find that he could see the monster's big nude butt. He banged on the creature's leg. "Move it, buddy."

The zeppelin's motor was fired. Steam kicked out of the boiler room, whistled whiteness into the wet night. The zeppelin jumped toward the sky, nearly jerking Hickok loose of the ladder.

Faster and higher the zeppelin went, the ladder with Bull, Hickok and the creature, flapping like clothes on a wash line. Arrows buzzed all around them.

Then the zeppelin was too high for arrows. The camp lights receded. Turning, Hickok could see the airfield, the planes there outlined by lanterns and fire pots. Half a dozen of the little Japanese hornets rose up in the airfield light, dissolved into the darkness. Hickok could hear them buzzing.

Hickok prodded the creature again, and he began to climb. Bull had long ago reached the top, was looking over the railing, calling to the creature. "Green face. Get move on."

The creature had to work carefully to free its wood block foot from the ropes with each step, but finally it reached the railing, and Bull, with the help of Cetshwayo, pulled him on board.

Hickok was swinging back and forth as the storm increased in savagery and the zeppelin rose faster and higher.

Cetshwayo and Bull began pulling the ladder up. Eventually, Hickok rolled over the railing and collapsed on the promenade deck. He sat up, and removed the arrow from his pants leg.

Buntline appeared on deck, a clutch of Winchesters under his arm. He passed them to Hickok, Annie, Bull, and Cetshwayo.

"You, physician fella. Get that damn green man inside."

The Master Physician grabbed the monster at the elbow, led him off the promenade, onto the enclosed deck. Through the great glass windows he could see the vague shapes of the biplanes in the darkness.

Annie was the first to fire. Her shot, as always, was a good one. She hit a pilot in his cockpit. The plane jerked, dove. Moments later there was an explosion and a flash of light as the biplane slammed into the shore near the Pacific ocean.

THE BIPLANES WERE TRAILING THE DARK CIGAR SHAPE, firing their simple guns. *Blat*. A beat. *Blat*. A beat. *Blat*. The guns were designed to fire with the beat of the propeller, slicing through at the precise moment of the blades' spacing. It was clever. It was tricky. And it didn't always work.

Hickok was glad they were not the new German planes which fired dual Gatling guns as fast as they could work till the ammunition ran out.

On the downside for them, the zeppelin had no real maneuverability. They were like a dying albatross besieged by falcons.

Wood splintered on the promenade deck, bullets pocked, cracked, or exploded glass on the main deck. One bullet went through the glass, drove splinters into the creature's face. A bullet tore through his upper left arm.

He didn't bleed.

Another bullet took Buntline's bowler hat, caused him to prostrate himself on the deck. The monster stood his ground, glass dangling from his chest. His kimono was torn and burned where the bullet had ripped through it and through his arm.

The planes were attacking the zeppelin itself. Bullets slammed into the great rubber casing, and though it was designed to take terrific impact from hail, flying birds, and small arms fire, the heavy bullets were succeeding in pounding through.

Hickok heard a hissing sound as the zeppelin let loose some of its helium. The good news was the big bag was actually a series of smaller gas cells. It could lose considerable helium and still stay airborne. The bad news was there was a limit to anything.

A biplane passed in front of the promenade deck. Bull shot it the finger, then they all raised their Winchesters and fired at its rear end.

Their shots smacked into the biplane's tail assembly. A stream of fire raced along the fuselage, rolled around the plane as if it were a hoop the craft were jumping through. Then the flames grabbed at the seat and the pilot, burst him into a human torch. The plane spun. The blazing pilot freed himself from his seat, and even as the plane turned over and over, he dropped free, a burst of meteoric flame driven hard into the ocean.

The plane exploded on the water. Flames spread on the surface, waves leapt wet and fiery until the fuel burned itself out.

The zeppelin sailed along rapidly, propelled not only by its motors, but by a strong tail wind. The Japanese pilots no longer exposed themselves to the zeppelin's defenders; they knew how unerringly accurate they were. Instead, they flew high above it, firing at the defenseless structure of the craft, causing it to collect damage.

ON THE ZEPPELIN'S BRIDGE, pilot William Rickenbacher, needed more steam. He was not used to working without a copilot, but Cody had insisted on a skeleton crew. William felt sick. Why had he agreed? Cody had given him a choice. He could have gone back with the others. His copilot, Manfred Von Richthofen, had been eager enough. But no. He wouldn't let him. He didn't want a dumb kid in command of his ship. Wanted to spare him the danger. What an idiot he had been. He had a wife and children. This was idiotic. He wasn't a spy, and he wasn't a fighter pilot. He was the captain of a luxury air ship.

Jesus. What had he been thinking?

Had he been thinking?

Not only were the biplanes tearing his craft apart, the storm was slamming it about. He was no longer sure of the difference between sea and sky. The only thing to do was to try and let the ship rise, propel it forward with full throttle.

"Gib eet more steam," he called through the command tube, trying to shape his words careful, so his heavy German accent would not be misunderstood. "Gib eet more steam. Power ees dying. Ve are losing altitude."

IN THE STEAM ROOM THE WORKERS STRUGGLED VALIANTLY with coal scoops and chunks of wood, tossed them into the great oven. The heat was unbearable. Steam hissed. Motors hummed. Men groaned. The ship moved slightly faster, rose gradually.

A BIPLANE BUZZED THE BRIDGE. William saw it as it passed. A moment later it turned in the darkness, came back. It fired a shot that blew out a fragment of the glass. Cold air embraced William, the blast nearly knocked him down. He turned, could see the plane's shape, flying fast toward him.

In that moment he knew there was no time to do anything, knew what was about to occur. His last thought was not of God, but of his wife Elizabeth, and his children, especially his favorite child, his little boy Eddie.

Then a bullet spat from the biplane, zipped through the already destroyed window, caught Richenbacker in the throat, opening a wound that looked like two rose petals falling apart. He fell face forward against the control console, blood rushing over the gears and dials.

Before William's corpse fell against the panel, the biplane's pilot realized he was in trouble. In getting close to the zeppelin's bridge, he had not allowed himself enough time to turn. He didn't even pretend to work the control stick. The pilot threw his hands over his eyes as the plane struck the command deck, knocked off the propeller, and was driven into the side of the zeppelin like a dart. The front of the plane rubbed William's body into a red smear. Fuel dripped from the damaged plane, trailed into the night air. Some of it dripped along the floor of the command deck, ran toward the door, slipped under the crack, fled along the corridor, was absorbed by the carpet.

When the plane struck the zeppelin, there was such a jerk, on the promenade, Captain Jack was tossed forward. He caught the rail, and just when it looked as if he would regain his balance, the zeppelin lurched once more, and Captain Jack went over the side and was silently swallowed by darkness.

Hickok tried to grab him as he went, but it was too late. The zeppelin tilted dramatically. All the defenders were tossed about. They struggled valiantly to hang on, grabbing at the rail, scratching at the promenade deck with their nails.

Buntline felt himself flying forward, toward the broken window on the main deck. He knew he was a goner. Through the gap in the glass he went, out into blackness. But just when he was trying to remember the Lord's prayer and decide if there was time to say it before he was splattered all over the Pacific, his jacket collar was snagged, and he was jerked inside, tossed on the floor.

Buntline looked up to see the creature looking down on him with a solemn expression.

"Thanks, old boy," Buntline said. "You're peachy by me."

Frankenstein's creation did not reply.

IN CODY'S CABIN, the collision of the plane hurled his head off its perch on the dresser. Had it not hit Goober in the side of the head, knocking him down, it might have smashed against the wall.

The jar lay on its side, the liquid in it sloshing. Cody yelled through the tube. "Get me up. Get me out in the open where I can die like a man."

Goober, a knot forming on his head, put one hand to his wound, got his feet under him. He picked up Cody's head, tucked it under his arm, darted out into the slanting hallway.

"Check the bridge," Cody said.

Goober rushed forward, his head feeling as if it were giving birth to a child. When he reached the hallway that led to the bridge, he could smell the fuel from the Japanese plane. He hustled along, feeling colder as he went.

When he reached the bridge, he saw a lumpy red smear that might have been Rickenbacker. It was smeared all over the console. The Japanese plane's nose was poked through the side of the zeppelin, and the pilot lay slumped in his seat. A freezing spray was blasting in from the outside.

"Goddamn," Cody said, when Goober turned his head upright, moved the jar around so he could see.

"We're done," Goober said.

"Hush your mouth, shorty. You are not dead till you're dead. And you do not quit till you quit. I thought I was dead when I fought my duel with Yellow Hand. He was a tough customer. I was about ready to give up and die. But something in me said, 'Don't do that, Buffalo Bill. You stick in there.' So, I stayed with it. Yellow Hand slipped on his own knife, stabbing his ownself to death. You got to stay with things. You never know how they will work out."

"I got a pretty good idea," Goober said.

"Quick," Cody said. "Back to my cabin."

"I thought..."

"Just do it!"

Out on the promenade deck, the zeppelin began to roll back level. The Japanese planes were now closing for the kill. Bullets slammed the deck from all directions. Cetshwayo took a shot in the side, let out a yell.

Annie and Hickok grabbed him under the arms, hauled him onto the main deck, laid him down. As they did, a plane came by so close its dual wings edged only six feet from the promenade railing.

Bull, the only one left on the railing, slammed several shots from his Winchester into it as it retreated. At first he thought he had failed. Then the plane's motor cut and there was a whistling sound as it went into a dive. This was followed by an explosion and a flash of light.

Glancing over the railing to see if planes might be coming up from below, Bull was greeted with the sight of the glowing, dangling ladders.

"Damn," he spoke to himself. "That how them follow so easy in dark. See ladders."

Bull tossed the Winchester to his left hand, pulled his knife from under his jacket, moved around the railing hacking the ladders free.

The steam man had a fire in its belly. Cody had ordered it kept going until they were out of this business. He wasn't sure what he might need the steam man for, but he wanted to be prepared.

His jar fastened to the steam man, Goober inside to work the controls, Cody returned to the bridge. Calling commands to the midget, the powerful steam man's body shoved at the plane. The pilot, who they thought was dead, lifted his head just as the steam man managed to shove the plane through the wound it had made in the zeppelin's side.

"Sayonora," Cody said.

The Japanese just looked sad as the plane fell backwards, said in Japanese, "Typical."

Cody, Goober, and the steam machine were hurled backwards as the zeppelin, relieved of the plane's weight, leapt skyward.

OUT ON THE PROMENADE, Bull was slammed face down on the deck so hard his nose bled. Inside the main deck, the zeppelin's defenders experienced the same moment of surprise.

The advantage, although not immediately known, was that the zeppelin was now lost to the biplanes. They could no longer see it in the dark and the rain. They were also running out of fuel, so there was nothing left for them to do but turn back.

The downside was the zeppelin had suffered many wounds in its rubber skin. Helium had been lost. The bridge was damaged. The zeppelin had no pilot. The steam man had been damaged by the sudden rise of the ship; it had caused the steam man's legs to crimp, and it had fallen. Somehow, Goober had gotten the front of his trousers hung up. As the machine lay on its side near the gap in the wall, Goober said, "I'm coming out of this thing, Cody. I'm jammed up in here. It's pinching my pee-pee."

Goober worked the trap door open, tore the front of his trousers loose and slipped out on the floor. He hastened to unfasten the clamps that held Cody's head in place. Finished, he clutched the jar under his arm as they stood looking at the wheezing steam man lying on its side.

Cody, peering through the glass, said, "I'm gonna miss that dude."

"Not me," said Goober. "It pinched my pee-pee. And it's hot. And it's hard work, too."

"Give me a crank, will you?"

BELOW IN THE BOILER ROOM all was panic. The great furnace had been in the process of being loaded when the plane came loose and the zeppelin jumped. Flaming hunks of wood and coal had been tossed from the furnace; the three men in the boiler room were frantically attempting to put out the flames with small tanks of water.

It was pointless.

The zeppelin dropped as if the bottom had come out of the world, and the ocean, like rolling concrete, came up to meet it on the way down.

Fall of the Zeppelin

WHEN THE ZEPPELIN HIT THE STORMY SEA the hot furnace exploded. Flames danced on the water, then hissed out, leaving boiling white smoke, charred lumber and stinking rubber in its wake. Waves crunched the decks and cabins, wadded up what was left of the helium filled tubing as if it were onion skin paper. The rain cried on the remains. Lightning slashed yellow sabre cuts across the sky.

The corpses of the boiler room workers, par-boiled, popped to the top, bobbed on the waves like corks. Floating with them was the jar containing Cody's head. He was cursing violently, calling for Goober.

The waves shoved Cody up, dropped him in a trough of foaming water; he saw the corpse of Goober float by face down. Then the whitecaps turned his jar and tossed him; water ran down the speaking tube, joined the mixture inside his container. Cody licked at the water. Salty, of course. But it did kind of neutralize the pig urine.

For once, Cody was glad he didn't have a stomach; all he could feel was a kind of dizziness.

Nearby, clinging to planks, were Hickok, Annie, and Bull. Cetshwayo and Frankenstein's monster were nowhere to be seen.

THERE WERE OIL-FUELED FLAMES burning on the water. In the light they provided, Hickok, clasping his plank, saw the others. The dead boiler room workers, Goober popping about, Annie and Bull clinging to a plank together, and finally, the head of Cody, surfing the waves in his sturdy Mason jar.

Hickok paddled over to Bull and Annie, pulled his bowie knife from its scabbard, stuck it in his plank, said, "Bull, we got to get hold of Cody, then find a way to lash some of this junk together."

Bull nodded.

Hickok swam to Cody's jar, grabbed it, swam it over to Annie. Then he and Bull set about building a raft. It was tedious, but by dog paddling about, grabbing planks and cutting strips of floating rubber, they were able to fasten a half dozen pieces of wood together.

By the time they finished jerry-rigging a raft, got Annie and Cody loaded on it, they were exhausted; the sun was burning through the haze, the rain was dying out, and the ocean was beginning to settle. Then the sharks came.

Hickok said, "No rest for the wicked, and the good don't need any."

Unconsciously, Hickok reached for his guns. But his sash was empty. They had been lost. He had even lost the bowie knife.

There were about a dozen of the beady-eyed bastards, circling the makeshift craft. One of them came near, rolled on its side, showed its dark dead eyes. It opened its mouth to reveal a hunk of dark flesh dangling from its teeth. Part of an arm actually. They recognized it. It belonged to Cetshwayo.

"That not good," Bull said.

Cody, in his jar, was singing drinking songs.

"He's starting to lose it," Hickok said.

"It's the salt water in the jar, mixed with his chemicals," Annie said. "And he could use a crank."

Hickok cranked him.

Cody went silent for a moment. Hickok held the jar in his lap, tilting it so he could look down into Cody's face.

"It's all right, pard. Or as good as it could be under the circumstances." Hickok turned the jar so Cody could see the contents of the raft. "We're the only survivors."

"All I want is a body so I can fight," Cody said. "If I can go down fighting, I'm all right."

Hickok placed Cody in the center of the raft, leaned back, waited for it to get hot and unbearable. He thought of food briefly, thought of water longer, then the flames on the water died and the sun rose high and hot and their flesh began to burn. The water in Cody's jar began to bubble.

ANNIE THOUGHT OF FRANK. For a long moment she remembered how he held her. Hickok held her, too. He was a passionate lover. But there was an urgency about him, a desire to get on with the act. Frank wasn't like that. He was slow about his business. God, she missed him.

56

She opened her eyes, looked at Hickok. He had his eyes closed. His long hair was wet and matted. His clothes clung to him, drying slowly in the sun. She thought he was gorgeous.

She closed her eyes, tried to grab back her memories of Frank. But this time, they wouldn't come. She thought of Hickok again, back on the zeppelin, in her cabin, in her bed.

BULL LOOKED OUT AT THE GREAT EXPANSE OF WATER and thought of the Greasy Grass. Greasy Grass was what his people called the Little Big Horn, where Custer and his soldiers died. The Greasy Grass had looked like a sea of grass, and this ocean, right now, looked much the same way.

The Greasy Grass. What a fight.

Bull thought: Bad day for white guys. Big day for red guys.

He wished he had participated, but it was over by the time he tried to join the fight. He had always felt slighted by that.

Bull closed his eyes, saw Crazy Horse standing before him, wearing only a loin cloth, lean and strong with braided hair. He wore warpaint. Spots on his body. He had the corpse of a hawk fastened to the side of his head.

He thought of how Crazy Horse had died. Held by his own people, bayonetted by soldiers.

"Sorry, friend," he said softly in Sioux. "I will soon join you."

BUFFALO BILL DREAMED OF WOMEN. All the women he had known and loved. He dreamed last of Lily Langtry. Her long white limbs, her thick dark hair, the darker patch between her legs.

God, at least Louisa could have let him finish. She already had him dead to rights. What would another half a minute have mattered?

Ooooh, that was one evil woman.

Yeah. He had made up his mind. He got out of this pickle, he was divorcing that bitch.

BY MIDDAY THE SHARKS HAD BECOME SO BOLD it was necessary to use one of the two planks they had kept for paddles to fight them off.

All Hickok could think of was one of them coming up from below, hitting the center of their leaky, poorly lashed raft, sending them all into the ocean to be sorted out by hungry sharks.

The evil fish came more often. Hickok and Bull fought them back constantly, banging at their snouts, poking at their eyes. Bull wounded one of them bad enough it bled. The others turned on it, biting, ripping, pulling at strands of gut.

"Maybe reservation not such bad idea after all," Bull said. "Wish Bull fat ass there. Not here."

"I'd rather fight a whole parcel of Sioux than deal with this," Hickok said. "No offense."

"Fuck you, Hickok."

The day burned on. They ached from thirst. Then, as night was about to fall, they saw the fin of an enormous shark.

No. A whale.

But whales didn't have fins like that.

Huge. Slicing the water like some kind of prehistoric fish, speeding directly toward them.

Rising from the water, spilling bubbles over its side, it revealed a long snout and bulbous black eyes. The brute crackled with illumination.

"What are you waiting for," Hickok yelled at it. "Eat us or go away."

The strange beast made a creaking noise. A flap opened in its top and, like Jonah freed, a man scrambled out of it. He was lanky, bearded, wore sailor style clothes and a fur cap. He had a large revolver strapped to his hip. His arms hung impossibly long by his sides.

"Ahoy," he said in an exotic voice. "You people seem in a bad way."

THE INSIDES OF THE GREAT FISH HUMMED. Behind them lay the eyes of the fish, which were actually a great, tinted, double-bubbled water shield. Before them was a long hall.

The sailor who had spoken to them and helped them onto the craft, sealed the round lid above them with a twist of a wheel. Two more sailors appeared. They looked just like the first sailor. Lanky, hairy, and long-armed. Close up, it was revealed they did not wear beards at all. Nor were those things on their heads hats. It was part of their heads. They had sharp teeth. They seemed to be large monkeys with a good backbone.

They were carrying white fluffy robes. The first drew his revolver and pointed it at them.

"Put them on," he said.

"The guns aren't needed," Hickok said.

The one with the gun ignored him, said, "Take off your clothes. Put the robes on."

"I beg your pardon," Annie said.

"We will avert our eyes," the sailor said.

"Like hell you will," Hickok said.

The sailor pointing the pistol cocked it. "Please," he said.

Bull and Hickok, Cody's head under his arm, turned their backs for Annie while she undressed and slipped on the robe. Next, passing Cody's head to Annie, Hickok and the others slipped on their robes.

Later, Annie admitted that the sailors had been most polite, actually averting their eyes while she changed. Hickok thought they were certainly unlike any sailors he had ever heard of.

Once in the robes, the sailors escorted them down a long hallway tricked out in thick red carpet. They entered a large room that housed a magnificent library; the smell of books was rich, laced with the stench of cigars, a bit of spilled whiskey, a hint of perspiration and the stout stink of fish. There was a soft looking red velvet couch and cushioned chair, a mahogany desk and a wooden chair. And the source of the fish smell.

A seal was perched in the stuffed chair, tail curled, holding a book with its flippers. It wore glasses on its nose, and a large, square, metal hat. It was obviously engrossed, flicking not a whisker or turning its head to observe them. Beside it, in a bowl, were the remains of a several sardines—heads and fins.

As they watched, one of the seal's flippers, moved, turned a page.

Bull, Annie, and Hickok looked at one another, looked back at the seal. Hickok, who had ended up with Cody's head, lifted the jar so Cody could see what they saw.

"You don't see that often," Cody said.

"I think he's actually reading that book," Annie said. "And it looks as if he has thumbs on his flippers."

"Oh, I assure you," said a voice, "he is reading the book, and those are thumbs of a sort."

They turned, saw a tall gentleman dressed in a soft white shirt, blue velvet trousers, woven sandals. He was nice looking with wide-spaced eyes, a large forehead, dark skin, and silvery hair.

All of the sailors, save one, disappeared. The remaining sailor edged backwards out of the way, but at service. He was the sailor with the gun. He dropped it by his side, but made no move to holster it.

"Ned, that's the seal, becomes deeply involved," the man said, "but the mere smell of a fresh fish will jerk him out of his concentration."

"What do seals read?" Hickok asked.

"Actually, his personal reading habits aren't up to snuff. He likes dime novels. *The Adventures of Buffalo Bill.*"

Bill cleared his throat. It sounded more like someone spitting water.

"Good Lord, is that a living head?" the man asked.

"I certainly am," Cody said. "I am Buffalo Bill Cody."

"No shit?"

"No shit."

The man took the jar from Hickok and examined it carefully. "You do look like him."

"It's him," Annie said.

The man gave the jar back to Hickok, studied Annie. "My, but you are lovely. And who are you?"

"I'm Annie Oakley, this is Sitting Bull, and Wild Bill Hickok."

"Well I will be twisted and peed on. I am honored. I know of all of you. My name is Bemo. Captain Bemo to my friends. This ship is my creation, the Naughty Lass.

Ned the Seal

"I named her that because she was a bitch to build," Bemo said. "My original name for her was Sea Shark, but no one in my original crew liked that one. Lots of grumbling about the name. I changed it to Nasty Sea Shark, but that didn't excite anyone either. I even considered The Real Nasty Sea Shark, but by that time I'd lost everyone. I should have just called it what I wanted. I didn't have to answer to anyone. Not then. But, I wanted to please. Finally, I decided on the Naughty Lass."

"By the way, we've heard of you, too." Hickok said. "And the Naughty Lass."

Neither Hickok nor the others mentioned Bemo had been considered a pirate, noted for destroying vessels on the high seas. It had been his way to combat war, destroying the ships that made war or carried goods for war. Every navy in the world put a price on Bemo and his ship, but the bounty came to naught. Since the attacks on ships ceased, it had been thought for the last few years that he had lost himself at sea.

"But you're supposed to be dead," Annie said.

"Don't believe everything you read," Bemo said. "And while I'm on the subject, there were some photos that got out. Me…unclothed, and well…I just want to say, if you saw those photos…Well, it was cold."

"Photos?" Annie asked.

"Taken by a disgruntled crew member. A female crew member, I hasten to add. I posed for them, caught up in the moment, you might say. Quite a mistake. They appeared in some French periodicals. So, again, don't believe everything you read, or see. In fact, I'm certain those photos were doctored. They can do that sort of thing, you know."

"Don't believe everything you read is right," Hickok said. "Including the stuff in Buffalo Bill dime novels."

"Some of it's real," Cody said. "And I thought it was Naughty Ass. Not Naughty Lass. I'm a little disappointed."

"Come," Bemo said. "Sit. I'll have food brought. All of it from the sea. Afterwards, seaweed cigars."

"I hate I'll miss that," Cody said.

"You're being snide," Bemo said. "But you really will miss out. This seaweed is high in nicotine. Quite tasty. Better than Cuban, actually. The only thing missing is it isn't rolled on the thighs of Cuban women. That's how it's done, you know."

"If that's true, I miss it already," Cody said. "The Cuban cigars, that is."

"These were actually rolled on the thighs of my crew," Bemo said. "That's not something I like to consider while I'm smoking."

"By the way," Hickok said. "Who is your crew? They are unusual."

"Ugly," Bull said.

"Yes, they are," Bemo said. "They're monkeys. Or they were. They have been altered through surgery, genetics, and chemicals. Their intelligence has been raised, and for the last twenty years or so, they, and…others, have been receiving training in all the basics. Reading, Writing, Arithmetic. The last part gives them trouble, but they try. I think their English is quite good, don't you? Come. Please. Take a seat."

The seal didn't give up his seat. He gave them a quick, uninterested glance, went back to reading.

There was plenty of room on the couch, and soon they were seated, telling their story, each filling in a little bit here and there.

"The Frankenstein creation," said Captain Bemo. "Ah, yes. I've heard of him. Lost to the waves, you say. Not exactly a pro-saic life, his, now was it? Or maybe it was overly prosaic. Depends on how you look at it, I suppose. Met the monster's creator once. Convention of inventors and scientists in Vienna. This was before he made news with his creation. Quite the bore, actually. Couldn't stop talking about anatomy, brains and vene-real disease. Had one, if I remember correctly. A venereal disease, of course. I'm sure you know he had anatomy and a brain, but the part about the disease, that is most likely news to you. Ghastly subject matter, venereal disease, isn't it?"

Annie said, "Thanks for rescuing us."

"When the storm finished I thought it would be more

energy-saving to travel on top of the sea, rather than under it. We found you entirely by accident. Think about that. We surface, and there you are. The proverbial needle in a haystack. Of course, since we weren't looking for you, you weren't even that. A happy accident. But this isn't exactly a rescue."

The zeppelinauts considered that statement, let it hang.

"About the seal?" Hickok asked. "I'm curious, is he just doing a trick? You were kidding about him reading, right?"

"Him like that hat?" Bull asked.

Bemo grinned. "That's not a hat. It's a brain enhancer. A bit of surgery was required, and now the brain, having grown to three times its size, needs more room. Thus, the hat, as you call it. Hat and brain have long since fused. The glasses are for bad eyesight, of course. And yes, he can read, and from the notes he takes, it's apparent he understands what he reads quite well. When left to his own devices, his reading habits are quite atrocious, but he can read heavier material if put to it. He's a good researcher. Takes insightful notes."

"Notes?" Annie said. "He can write?"

"It's a bit messy," Bemo said. "But legible. He's working on it. Wears a pad and pencil around his neck."

"Can he talk?" Hickok asked.

"Don't be ridiculous," Bemo said. "Isn't it enough he can read and write and use the toilet? He can stand a bit more upright than the average seal, however. He's had some adjustments. He does have a tendency to lose his glasses, and that's why we've added a chain to the ear pieces, so that he can hang it, along with his pen and pad, around his neck."

"You did that?" Cody asked. "Expanded his brain. Taught him to read."

"Oh, no. I'm talented. But my abilities tend to be more of the mechanical, ecological nature. This is the work of Doctor Momo."

"Momo?" Cody said. "I thought he might be dead."

Bemo grimaced. "No. He's quite alive, I assure you. Ned is sort of on loan to me. I have him read certain texts, evaluate them, write up his notes. He also takes dictation from me."

"What's he researching?" Annie asked.

"Material for Doctor Momo," Bemo said. "There are a number of items Momo needs for his experiments that only come from the sea. I acquire these for him, and do some research. With Ned's help, of course."

"I've wanted to meet Doctor Momo for some time," Cody said. "I have friends who would love to meet him as well. Sam Morse. Professor Maxxon. Chuck Darwin. Many others."

"My goodness," Bemo said. "Famous people, all. This is wonderful. Your friends may not get their wish, but you will, Mr. Cody. And the friends with you. You will meet him. We are, in fact, on our way to Momo's island."

"You're jerkin' me," Cody said.

"As how there's little to jerk," Bemo said, "I doubt that. And by the by, how did that happen, good man? The head business and the jar, I mean?"

"Cut myself shaving," Cody said.

"Very well, your business," Bemo said. "No need to discuss it."

"And you're not jerking me about Doctor Momo?"

"I said as much. And beyond the physical, neither am I jerking you in a figurative sense. We are indeed on our way to see Doctor Momo."

"I suppose you two are great friends," Annie said.

"No, actually, I hate the sonofabitch, but..." Bemo stood from his place on the couch, turned to reveal the back of his head.

It was missing. A large chunk of hair and skull had been removed. There was a shiny bulb screwed into his brain, the gray matter around it pulsed.

When Bemo turned to face them, he said, "You see, I'm in a bit of a pickle. Wrecked the Naughty Lass on his island once. I was grievously injured in the wreck. My crew was killed. Doctor Momo saved me. But, knowing who I was and what I could do for him, he cut out a bit of my brain, fastened in an apparatus that makes me submissive to him and in need of frequent bowel movements. I talk a little fruity, as well. I'm a kind of zombie."

"Good Lord," said Cody.

66

"Yes," Bemo said. "And in short time you will meet my master. And you won't like it that much, I assure you. An absolute asshole, Momo. Absolute."

THE RESCUED ZEPPELINAUTS spent the night in comfort in separate cabins, Cody's head in the library on a shelf. In spite of Bemo's disconcerting revelations about the zombie business and the comment about them not going to like Momo, for the first time in three days, mostly due to exhaustion, they slept well and awoke rested.

During the night their clothes had been cleaned and dried, left folded at their bedsides before morning. Annie had been supplied with a large box of brushes, combs, and hair pins. She used them minimally, looking lovely with little effort.

Early morning, for their benefit, just before arrival at the island, Bemo had taken the Naughty Lass down. They stood at the great water shield and watched. Hickok held Cody's jar. The sea foamed about the nose of the sub, then overwhelmed it. They dropped deep, burned a bright exploratory light that revealed all manner of fish and water creatures. They saw reefs. They saw shipwrecks.

"I really would like to have shown you Atlantis," Bemo said, "but, alas, we are nowhere near it, and I'm afraid I don't choose for myself much anymore. You know how it is, the bulb and all."

An hour before they reached the island, a breakfast was provided. There was stewed kelp, salmon, fish eggs and kippers. There was a kind of coffee made from dried seaweed. There was bread ground from an underwater plant. It was all delicious. Cody, unable to eat, was the table centerpiece.

A mile out from the island, they surfaced. The Naughty Lass entered the island of Doctor Momo via an inlet bordered on both sides by a monkey- and parrot-filled jungle.

Bemo allowed them on the sea-slick deck of the Naughty Lass as they sailed in. Hickok carried Cody's head. Bull watched the monkeys leaping and chattering with the same deadpan expression as always. Blue and red parrots exploded from the jungle, water birds burst toward the sky in blues, whites and grays. Huge water snakes were spotted.

Bull blinked once, having thought he saw a female head poke from the water, but when he looked again, there was only a huge fish tail flipping up and dropping away.

Annie had Ned the seal at her side. She had tried to pet and coo to him the night before, but the seal wasn't having any until she explained the head in the jar was that of Buffalo Bill, the hero of the dime novels Ned loved. After that, the seal was her companion.

Annie attempted to introduce Ned to the head of his hero, but Ned was too nervous. Hero worship prevented it. But he had taken to carrying a copy of one of Buntline's dime novels under his flipper. It was titled *Buffalo Bill's Journey to the Centre of the Earth*. Also included, *Richard, Lord of the Jungle, or, the Swinging Dick*.

Upon arriving at the dock, they were greeted by a strange sight. A hunchback and a metal man.

"We have a welcoming party," Hickok said.

"Yes," Bemo said. "I used the Marconi Wave to send news ahead."

The hunchback was excessively hairy. His face was dark with it. Hair pushed out of the back of his shirt and through the front where it buttoned. He scuttled hurriedly onto the deck as if he might be receiving candy. He had a wandering eye, a left foot larger than his right, a buck-toothed smile, and a less than conventional dress pattern. He wore a white shirt, a bow tie and a jet-black bowler hat and thatched sandals. He seemed nervous, as if ants had taken to his rectum.

The metal man was even more amazing. Sleek, well formed, his face appeared to have been modeled after the Greek god Apollo. He flashed in the sun like a rifle barrel. Like the hunchback, his manner of dress was unusual. He wore a pair of knee-length red shorts, a black vest that was wide open, revealing his rippled blue-metal stomach and swollen chest. He had pink painted toenails.

A chain was fastened to the left side of the vest; it stretched across the gap, where it disappeared into the right vest pocket;

the pocket bulged with the shape of an enormous turnip watch; it could be heard ticking, like the beating of a small tin drum.

"Oh," said the hunchback. "What we got here? Oh, my goodness, she's so lovely. You're a lovely, lovely lady."

When he spoke there was a chattering to his voice, as if he had learned English from monkeys.

Annie smiled. "Thank you, sir. And your name?"

"Jack. At your service." He scooped the bowler off his head, bowing low. "May I escort you to shore?"

"That would be most gracious," Annie said.

Ned took her hand in his mouth, began to lead her toward the dock.

"Ned!" Jack said. "I just offered my services."

Ned paid no attention. With Annie laughing, he guided her off the boat, onto the dock. Jack followed, paying close attention to the swing of Annie's ass.

Hickok shifted Cody to the crook of his left arm, and out of habit, reached to touch the butts of his guns.

Of course, there was nothing there.

Warily, he proceeded ashore.

As Bull stepped off the submarine with Bemo, he said, "Any place to do business?"

"Business?" Bemo asked.

"Number two?"

"Number what?"

"Shit? Need shit."

"Oh, why yes. I'll show you one of the outdoor facilities."

THEY WERE LED TO A GREAT HOUSE made of native logs and thatch. It was stately, two stories, surrounded by a compound with palisades and a massive gate.

There were inhabitants in the fort. They were monkey men. No monkey women were visible.

The Wild Westers were given rooms. Annie and Hickok insisted on a room together, and their wish was granted. Cody also had a room. He was placed on a dresser with the back of his head to the mirror; seeing his head floating in a jar was just too much for the vain Cody and he insisted he be placed that way.

Heated water was brought in and poured for baths by the monkey people. White cotton trousers and a white jacket were supplied for Bull, Hickok, and Annie. There were also little cotton shoes with thatch soles.

Cody's jar was cleaned and the big tin lid was polished.

Their doors were locked from the outside.

Late in the day, their doors were unlocked by the metal man, who told them in his metallic voice that his name was Tin. He carried Cody, led the others along a corridor and into a fine dining room that connected to a sunlit veranda, a long table and tall-back chairs.

Ned, the seal, waddled into the room, and when he saw Buffalo Bill being carried by the Tin Man, he brightened. Bemo followed shortly behind, looking pleasant enough for a man with a pulsing bulb in the back of his brain.

At the table, Tin introduced them to the middle-aged, gray-haired Momo who was already seated, dressed in white cotton shirt and trousers, drinking a very dark wine, spots of which dotted the front of his shirt. He smiled at them with gray, slightly bucked teeth in a tan face. His eyes looked like the ass end of silver bullets.

Tin guided each of the guests to their seat. Hickok was on the left of Momo, Annie the right. Cody's head was placed in the middle of the table, and Bull was placed at the far end, facing Momo. Bemo sat next to Bull. Tin and Ned did not take a seat. They stood near the edge of the veranda, watching and waiting.

A moment later, Jack scuttled into the room, scraping and shuffling, his bowler hat in his hand. With him came a faint aroma that might have been dung and sweat sweetened with urine.

"Sorry I'm late, Doctor," Jack said. "So sorry."

"Very well," Momo said. "Tell Catherine she may serve now."

"Yes, Doctor," Jack said, put on his bowler and scuttled from the room. When he returned a moment later, he removed his hat, squatted next to Momo's chair.

70

The meal was served by an attractive woman with thick black hair. She was short and well built and had a curious way of moving. Her eyes were bright green and her mouth was broad and thick lipped. She wore a short yellow dress. It was just to her knees and the boots she wore were black and laced and very tiny.

Catherine moved quickly and carefully until everyone was served. When she bent to serve him, Hickok noted that she had a pleasant musky aroma about her.

Finished, she disappeared from the room, silent as a cat.

The food, though tasty in design, was hard to consume because of Momo's dining habits.

The hunchback sat in a chair next to Momo and fed him his dinner bite by bite with a long wooden fork. Sometimes, if the meat being served was not tender enough, the hunchback pre-chewed it for Momo, placed it on the fork when it was properly soft and soggy, and fed it to the good doctor.

Even Bull—who had eaten grubs and maggots, boiled dogs and raw buffalo livers, picked corn kernels out of horse shit, and was accustomed to poking food into his mouth with his fingers—was appalled.

"I am most glad to have you here as guests," Momo said with a jaw full of food, then stopped suddenly, reached a probing finger into his mouth, pulled out a wad of graying meat. "This still has gristle," he said to Jack.

"Sorry, Doctor," Jack said, took the food from Momo's finger, poked it into his own mouth, began chewing vigorously.

While Jack was at work on the meat, Momo said, "This island is my island, and I welcome you. Of course, you won't be leaving."

"And what's to stop us?" Cody asked.

"Tin," Momo said sharply. "Come in here, please."

The metal man stepped forward. Momo said, "Demonstrate."

Tin picked up one of the empty chairs, wadded it into curled splinters with a slight movement of his hands.

"He can also run fast, see extreme distances, and for reasons I won't go into here, he's very dedicated to me. There are also other obstacles you would face escaping from this island.

My servants and guards. The ocean itself. It's best just to be comfortable."

At that moment, Catherine, the servant, reappeared with a tray containing dessert and coffee. She set both in the center of the table, poured each of them a cup of java, served them heavy devil's food cake and left the room. As she passed, Doctor Momo patted her on the behind.

"Good girl," he said.

Hickok said, "We would prefer to leave, Doctor."

"I'm afraid I must insist," Momo said. "Nothing bad will come of you if you stay. I mean, in one shape or fashion you will carry on. It's not so horrible here. We have a large house, plenty of rooms, built by the island's labor. And I believe you will find me an amusing host."

"I'm already amused," Annie said.

"Good," Momo said.

"Who are these islanders?" Cody asked.

"Actually, when I arrived, this island was populated only by animals."

"You're saying they are your creations?" Cody said.

"Very astute," Momo said, lifting a hip, cutting a fart sharp enough to use as a bread knife. "I've been most busy. Our servant, Catherine, or as I sometimes call her, Cat, was produced from a small species of wildcat on the island. Not a large cat, I might add. But look at her now."

"Ridiculous," Annie said.

"And Jack here. He was once a chimpanzee." Momo reached out and tapped Jack on the head. Jack smiled, and for the first time they could see that his teeth had been filed off to appear more human.

"All right," Annie said. "In his case, I believe it."

"I am aware of your work," Cody said. "But I've never heard that you actually created human beings."

"You're aware of my old work, Mr. Cody. It is nothing compared to what I'm doing now. Captain Bemo told me of your friends. Samuel Morse. Professor Maxxon. Who else? Darwin? I understand you also had in your possession Frankenstein's creation."

Catherine

"That's correct," Cody said.

"A shame you lost the creature. I'm sure it would have made quite a toy for the island. And these friends of yours, Morse, Maxxon. Good minds compared to yourself and the average moron, but compared to mine, their brains are doo-doo."

"Doo-doo?" Hickok said.

"Yes, doo-doo," Momo said. "And this monster Frankenstein created...child's play. Nothing of real importance. Cobbling a body out of corpses. That's not creation. That's re-creation. My work...that's creation. Tell them, Jack."

"It's very creative," Jack said.

"Damn, he's cute," Momo said. "I love this guy. I can remember a time when he only ate bananas and played with his balls. But look at him now. He looks near human. Ugly, but human. Still, look at him. He doesn't just eat bananas now. Eats meat as well. Still plays with his balls, but you can't accomplish everything in one fell swoop."

"What we would like," Annie said, "is for you to allow Captain Bemo to deliver us home. That is all we ask. Once we arrive, we would be glad to pay you for your inconvenience."

"Ah, my beautiful Little Miss Sure Shot. Your reputation precedes you, and I would be very amused to see you shoot sometime, and I would very much like to see you with your naked butt turned over a log, but, I cannot let you go."

Hickok jumped to his feet. "Don't you dare speak to her that way. I challenge you to back up your mouth, Mister. Guns. Knives. Bare hands."

"I'll use Tin," Momo said.

Tin slapped Hickok on the shoulder, knocking him to the ground.

"Sorry about that," Momo said. "Tin, help him up."

"I can manage," Hickok said.

Tin pulled Hickok to his feet anyway, sat him in his chair. Annie leaned over, put a hand on Hickok's knee, whispered, "Take it easy. He's about a quart shy a gallon."

"The problem is," Momo said, "you will not forget you have been here. I know human nature better than that. Mr. Cody, wouldn't you like a body to go with that head? Wouldn't you want to see my research go on until I'm ready to reveal it to the world? Not have some do-gooder who thinks I am evil rush out here to the island to put a ruin to my work? Think of it. Goddamn Christians tromping around on this paradise. Destroying what I have accomplished. Putting up churches. Trying to teach my people about God. A fool's mission. I am not even sure they have souls."

"Fuck Christians," Bull said suddenly.

Everyone looked to the end of the table. Bull raised his drinking glass. "Death to Christians," he said. "Dirty shit-heads." Bull took a long pull at the wine in his glass.

"Well now, a kindred spirit," Momo said.

"No," Bull said, pouring himself more wine. "Bull not like Christians. Pretty much think you asshole."

"Honesty is the best policy," Momo said. Then to Cody: "But that body to go with your head. You would like it, would you not?"

"I would," Cody said. "In fact, I have a body. My old one. Back home. On ice. Powered by electricity and batteries. All that modern science allows keeps it alive, waiting until a method can be discovered for reconnecting my head to my shoulders."

"Why wait?" Momo said. "I can do it for you now."

"You can?"

"You bet your ass I can," Momo said. "Then again, you don't have an ass, do you?"

"You all ass," Bull said.

"Mr. Indian Man," Momo said, "do not push me."

Bull grinned.

"I do not want just any body attached to my head," Cody said.

"Posh. I do not work that way. I will grow you a body. From your own cells. It would be like the body you had before. Only younger. Stronger. It is no trouble. Not really. I have never done it before, of course. Not having any humans to work on, but I have done it with animals, and I'm ready to give it the old college try, and all that. I am certain I can do it. Whoa. Hold on."

76

Doctor Momo

Momo let a fart fly. Jack went to fanning immediately.

Annie said, "I hope you can grow some manners while you're at it."

"Understand, on this island I set the standards for behavior," Momo said. "And I delight in violating the old rules. Makes me feel in control, you know. Kind of a flaw actually, but there you have it. And you know what, young lady? I may just see you naked and bent over that log yet. In fact, I may brand you on the hip. A big fat M for Momo."

Angry, Hickok eyed Tin. Tin, as if reading his mind, was eyeing him. Hickok thought about it a moment, decided it was best to bide his time. He forced himself to turn his attention to dessert and coffee.

After his first forkful, he glanced at Bull. Bull had already eaten his dessert and was pouring himself more coffee. He seemed to have lost all interest in the conversation.

Bull was like that. Paid attention until it didn't seem necessary to pay attention anymore. Kept his feelings to himself most of the time, but now and then, as with his comments about Momo, he'd let an opinion loose.

Bull said, "Got cigar?"

Momo eyed Bull for a moment, then…"A proper suggestion," Momo said. "Bemo prepares these from seaweed."

"So we know," Hickok said, waving a hand at Bemo. "Why have you done…*this* to Bemo?"

"I found him and his sub in one of my coves. His crew was dead. Bemo was badly injured himself. The only survivor. The Naughty Lass had been injured badly as well. I, of course, knew about him, his activities on the high seas, his strong stance against war and all the machines of war. I didn't really give a shit about that, but I thought I could use him, so, I made some adjustments in his brain, as well as gave him medical attention. He got better, and I created a crew for him…literally. They were originally howler monkeys, every one of them. The island is covered in my monkey creations. All male. Bemo, like the monkey men, though less willingly, does my bidding. Correct, Bemo?"

"I'd rather not," Bemo said. "But yes."

"But yes," Momo repeated. "If he doesn't, I don't replace the special bulb in his gray matter on a regular basis, and he dies. I can control him quite easily if he becomes annoying, or decides, as now, to adopt a sort of smart attitude in his voice." Momo produced from his pocket a chain, and what looked like a watch.

"No," Bemo said.

Momo pressed the device. Bemo screamed, fell out of his chair, onto the floor.

"I will be good. I will be good." Bemo repeated over and over.

Momo ceased pressing the watch. "Careful, Bemo, you'll burst your bulb on the floor there, and that wouldn't be good. And you are damn right you will be good. Jack, see to some cigars. Get a big fat one for Bemo. I have a feeling he'll need it. Miss Oakley? A cigar for you? Any kind at all. You know what I mean. You know of Freud, do you not? A real cigar? A symbolic one that I personally can provide?"

"No thank you," Annie said.

Ned, who had stood silent near Annie, eased forward, touched her elbow with his cold nose. When she looked down at him, she could see he was trembling and there were tears in his big black eyes.

The Wild Westers were given limited run of the island. They could visit one another in their rooms during the day, could venture about the house and veranda, but were not to go upstairs to Momo's private quarters, nor were they to go to what Momo called the Barracks. This was a chain of small buildings at the edge of the compound where his "people" lived and where his laboratory was located. The laboratory he referred to as the House of Discomfort.

They also had access to the closest beach, but were asked not to wander off in the woods, or to the beach on the opposite end of the island.

A few days went by, and one night in their room, Hickok and Annie, having finished lovemaking, lay close and talked. "What kinds of wild animals would be on an island like this one?" Hickok asked.

"Pigs?" Annie said. "Rabbits. Squirrels, maybe."

"I suppose."

"Crocodiles possibly. Isn't there some kind of salt water crocodile?"

"I don't know," Hickok said. "I believe there is."

"Monkeys, of course. And parrots. Other kinds of birds. Snakes maybe. Rats. Ships could have brought in creatures like that. I would guess different kinds of lizards. Cats. He said Catherine was made of a wild cat, if you believe that."

"Why not? I believe he made those guards from monkeys. And Jack from a chimpanzee."

"I suppose you're right, but she looks to have been a more successful experiment. Wouldn't you say?"

"She's all right," Hickok said, giving the classic male answer when a female asks a man's opinion of the appearance of another female. He quickly changed the subject. "No big predatory cats would be here," Hickok said. "Regular ship cats were most likely marooned, mated, produced a wild species, but hardly anything life threatening to humans. Certainly not bears. Not on an island this small."

"So what are you saying?"

"I'm saying, Annie, that Momo admits to creating humans from animals, if you can call a creation like that human, but at worst, his source for these creations is house cats, monkeys, possibly wild hogs, or dogs. Nothing truly dangerous. But why would he not want us in the woods, or the far side of the beach? What could harm us?"

"The creations themselves?"

"We've seen them. Think about Bemo's sailors. Long arms. Very hairy. Didn't have sense enough to look at you when you were naked. They carry guns, but, unless given direct orders, they seem harmless enough. Not dangerous by nature."

"He said the one he calls Jack was developed from a chimpanzee. Could chimpanzees be deadly?"

"Probably brought the chimpanzee to the island himself. And I don't believe chimpanzees are by nature particularly dangerous. Unless provoked, that is? Again, I'm no animal expert, but I say what's to harm us? What's his fear? And does he truly care about our welfare? He doesn't strike me as all that worked up about anyone other than himself."

"Why does it matter?"

"Why wouldn't he want us to wander about other than our own protection? Could it be he fears we might find a way off the island? A boat perhaps. Is that what he's keeping us from?"

"So, of course, you want to investigate."

"Of course. But right now there's something else I'd like to investigate...a flat brown mole on the inside of your right thigh."

"That's not a mole."

"No?"

"Believe it or not, it's a powder burn."

"Say what?"

"I've only told Frank this, but when I was young, learning to shoot, I became enraptured with guns. I handled them like a gambler handles cards. Handled them nude even. I once had an old Colt revolver without a trigger guard, just had the trigger hanging out. I thought, what if I turned it upside down, between my legs, barrel pointing out like a man's...you know..."

"Johnson."

"Yes...well, I wanted to see if I could pull the trigger with the muscles in my...you know."

"Vagina."

"I believe I would have said the lips of my Venus Mound, but yes. And, I did."

"I'll be damned."

"But the barrel was short, the load was heavy, took a powder flash, burned a spot into my thigh and it's been there ever since."

"Did you hit the target?"

"I hate to report it was a miss...but the second time I tried it, I hit it. And I didn't burn myself."

"Can you still do it?"

"I don't know, I haven't tried it since. But you know what?"

"What?"

"There are other things I can do."

Hickok rolled on top of her, said, "I know that."

"Yeah, well, there are some things I know you don't know about. Yet."

"I doubt that."

"Years of marriage teaches possibilities."

"Show me."

She did. And she was right.

THAT AFTERNOON, OUT ON THE BEACH, Bull walked with Annie and Hickok. The seal followed from a distance, thinking itself hid. Ducking behind rises of sand from time to time, clumps of bush.

Hickok said to Bull, "We were thinking about violating Momo's orders."

"Bull good at no follow orders," Bull said. "Momo crazy white eyes. Like to cut him. Think it fun to scalp little man. Like his hat."

"Jack, you mean?" Annie asked.

"Ugh."

"It would look good on you, Bull," Annie said. "The hat. Not the scalp."

"Where Cody?"

"With Momo." Hickok said.

"Him need help?"

"His own choice," Annie said. "Maybe he thinks he can find out something that will help us if he buddies up to Momo. And I think he'd like a new body to go with that head."

"Can't blame him for that," Hickok said. "But I've known him a long time. He always comes around when the chips are down."

"Let's walk," Annie said.

"What about our tagalong?" Hickok said, jerking his head toward Ned.

"I think Ned likes us. Especially Cody. He reads the dime novels. All of us are in them. He idolizes us."

IN AN OUTBUILDING STUFFED WITH BEAKERS, test tubes, wires, lights, and colored liquids, Momo worked a booger free from his nose with a dirty finger, wiped it on his pants, said, "I doubt your friends understand what I'm trying to accomplish here, but you, Mr. Cody, being perhaps the most worldly of the bunch...I believe you must."

As Momo talked, Buffalo Bill's head was placed dead center of a long wooden table by Jack. The liquid in Cody's jar had changed colors, gone pale. Cody felt stranger than usual. The turning of the crank by Jack did little to stir the cobwebs in his brain. Cody was beginning to feel—and he had to laugh when he thought it—disconnected; as if his soul were being stretched like taffy.

He supposed there were a variety of reasons for this. The fouled liquid in his jar. The aging and watering of the mechanical devices attached to his neck; the wires that were traced to his brain; the unoiled mechanism of the crank.

At the table's end, directly in front of him, was a square glass receptacle placed on a six inch thick metal platform. The glass contained a howler monkey's head. The head was alive, juiced by a power pack situated on top of the container. From the power pack, cables ran into the side of the glass, plugged directly into the monkey's brain. There was no liquid in the container. The monkey looked alert. Its neck swiveled on a rotator.

"He can turn and look in different directions merely by stretching muscles in his neck and cheeks," Momo said. "It took a bit of effort to teach him, but a man could learn it rather quickly. An afternoon or two, would be my guess."

"And if you smile too hard," Cody said, his voice coming weakly through the speech tube, "do you spin about like a top?"

"It takes a special kind of effort. Not hard, but more effort than you would have smiling, or frowning. Or eating."

"Of course, the monkey doesn't eat," Cody said.

"Oh, he does," Momo said.

"But how? It would run into his neck, fill up...he can't."

"He can, and does. Jack!"

Jack scuttled about in the back, clanking this, clanking that, finally showed up with a flexible tube, fastened it to the sides of the metal platform; the opposite end of the tube was dropped into a metal container, a large can to be exact.

The front of the glass case was snapped free. Jack produced a wild plum, held it up to the monkey's mouth. The teeth snapped as Jack jerked the plum back. The monkey worked its mouth, frantic for the fruit.

"That is quite enough of that business, Jackie-Boy," Momo said. "Tease him when I'm not demonstrating. He has such fun with that silly monkey head."

Jack laughed, placed the plum so the monkey could eat it.

It gobbled hungrily as Jack moved his fingers out of the way of the monkey's teeth.

"This way," Momo said, "though the monkey has no stomach, it can taste the plum. The refuse runs through a gap in its neck, into the box on which the contraption rests. From there it's sucked out by the tubes and into the metal stomach, as I like to call it. Is that not some clever shit?"

The plum gone, Jack turned a key on the side of the box. It began to pump, pulling the plum refuse from the box and into the metal stomach. Cody could hear it plopping into the bottom with a thud.

"For the monkey, it doesn't matter," Momo said. "He doesn't need food. I give the head an injection daily. This injection provides all the nutrients the brain, the skin, the eyes need. The cables are there for extra help, but I've improved my work so much, he really doesn't need them. An electrical charge is no longer necessary…do you miss taste, Mr. Cody?"

"I do."

"I thought you might. Put the monkey away, Jack. In fact, get rid of it. I've had it long enough. Perhaps we'll have a new use for our apparatus. A more important one. Huh, Mr. Cody?"

Jack produced a screwdriver, unfastened the head from the platform, pulled it free of wires and tubes with a plopping sound. Holding the creature's head by its fur, Jack shoved the back door open, tossed the head up slightly, gave it a sharp kick, causing it to disappear into the distance.

"Plenty monkeys where that one came from," Momo said.

THEY WALKED ALONG THE BEACH, and as they walked the jungle to the left of them grew thicker and darker and the sounds from it intensified. The ocean crashed over the algae-covered rocks to their right, foamed around them, crashed against the beach.

They were soon past the point Momo permitted, and they kept walking.

The natural sandy beach changed, became more barren, narrow and rock laden. The jungle turned ever darker and thrived closer and closer to the sea. The sounds of birds and animals intensified.

Once, Hickok stopped suddenly, looked at what he thought was a face poking out of the foliage, but when he blinked, it was gone.

"Did you see that?" Hickok asked.

"What is it?" Annie asked.

"It looked like a wild hog, with large tusks, but…"

"But what?"

"Its face was nearly six feet off the ground. It had to be standing upright. But that can't be."

Bull grunted. "Was hog. Hog man. Saw it."

Hickok and Annie looked at Bull. Hickok said, "You saw it too?"

"Bull see."

"Maybe Momo did have a positive reason to keep us away from the jungle and the other side of the beach," Annie said. "Maybe he has other creations. Not so successful ones. He said something to that effect. I didn't realize he meant they were…out here."

"Could be," Hickok said, "but I'd still like to see the other side. I don't cotton to being stuck on this island forever. Not if I can find a boat. Or someone who can get us off."

"Perhaps we could take the Naughty Lass," Annie said.

"I wouldn't know how to control it," Hickok said. "We'd sink."

"Bemo might help us."

"Not with that thing in his head. He might want to, but there wouldn't be any way."

"Talk less," Bull said. "Walk more."

They continued along the beach, keeping a wary eye directed toward the jungle. In time they came to a wad of seaweed and driftwood on the beach. As they neared it, they saw something was entangled in it. It was a large man wearing the shreds of a Japanese kimono.

It was the Frankenstein monster, minus an arm. Like Cetshwayo, the sharks had torn it off. Unlike Cetshwayo, the monster had survived. The block of wood had been wrenched from its foot, and now there was only a nub of bone visible.

"My God," Annie said. "Is he…alive?"

"Fact is," Hickok said, "he was dead before he was what he is now. Whatever that is."

"Please see," Annie said.

Hickok went to check. He raked back some seaweed, touched the creature's neck. "No pulse," he said. "But I don't know that means anything."

It didn't. The monster slowly raised its remaining arm, opened its hand and clasped it over Hickok's.

"For lack of more accurate words," Hickok said, "it's alive."

BULL STAYED WITH THE MONSTER while Annie and Hickok returned to the compound. Momo was on the veranda sitting in a wicker chair, drinking a tall mint julep served by Catherine, the woman who had been a cat.

When Hickok told Momo what they had found, Momo's countenance clouded.

"You went beyond the point I asked of you," Momo said.

"It was an accident," Hickok lied. "We just got carried away. It was so beautiful. The weather was so nice. And then we saw the monster. I hope you'll forgive our trespassing."

"Very well," Momo said. But he didn't sound very forgiving.

MOMO SENT A RESCUE PARTY in a motorized vehicle. Behind the hooded motor was an enclosed, two-seat, black cab. Inside the cab rode Tin and Jack. Tin operated the craft with a stick he wobbled left and right; a pedal he pushed with his foot. At his left was a crank he used for a brake. The cab pulled a flatbed cargo carrier made of wood panels. Annie and Hickok rode on that. The vehicle moved an exciting five miles an hour on flat-rimmed metal wheels. The motor made a sound like something dying and whining in pain.

Eventually they came to the spot where Bull sat on a hunk of driftwood, and nearby the monster lay tangled in seaweed.

When the vehicle was stopped, Jack bounded over to the monster, sniffing the air. "He stinks. He stinks good."

When Tin saw the monster lying there, he startled so much his body made a noise like teapots slamming together. "He is so big."

"Yeah," Hickok said. "He's a big one."

"And he is made from the parts of other men?" Tin asked.

"That's the story," Hickok said. "And I believe it. In a way, he's not living at all. He moves. He thinks. But he's not really living."

"Neither am I," said Tin.

Hickok rapidly changed the subject. "Let's load him up."

They laid the monster on the flatbed, turned the vehicle around, started back. Bull joined Hickok and Annie on the bed with the monster.

They hadn't gone far when the creatures appeared.

THEY CAME OUT OF THE WOODS and stood in front of the vehicle, which Tin slowed to a stop just in time to keep from running over them. They didn't seem to realize that the vehicle could crush them. There were at least twenty of them, and shortly thereafter, twenty more. Their numbers kept increasing as they slipped from the woods to surround and crowd the vehicle.

They stood like men, wore rags of clothes, but were more animal in appearance than human. Theirs were the faces of hogs, dogs, goats, bears, cows, a lion, a wolf, and even one reptilian face. Some of them seemed to be two or three animals blended.

Yet, their bodies were different from their animal sources. There was a greater intelligence about them, a deeper curiosity. They ran their hands over the vehicle, sniffed at it. Their hands sometimes had five fingers and a thumb, sometimes not.

The Beast Men

Several of them climbed up on the wooden bed, sniffed at the prone body of the monster.

"We thought you were bringing us another man." said the one who looked like a wolf. His yellow eyes were intense, and his lips dripped foam. "We have not had a new man among us in some time."

Tin and Jack had gotten out of the truck. Jack was carrying a coiled whip in his hands. When the creatures saw it, they cowered instinctively.

"There is no man here," Jack said. "Not like you, anyway."

"Yes, this is another man," Tin said. "He has been hurt. We are taking him to the doctor."

"To the House of Discomfort?" asked the Wolf.

"No, Sayer of the Law," said Tin. "He is to be treated for wounds. He has done nothing wrong."

"And who are these men?" asked Sayer of the Law. "Are they the creations of the Lord Father?"

"Yes," Tin said quickly. "We are all the creations of the Lord Father Momo."

The wolf creature, Sayer of the Law, moved closer to Tin, said, "If this is so, and if this man," he gestured toward the unconscious monster, "is not of the Father, then who is he of? And if he is of other than the Father, then is the Father not the father of all?"

"He is," Tin said. "But there are some things too complicated to explain. He is the father of this man, as he is your father. That is all you need to know."

"Then if he is of the Father," said the Sayer of the Law, "and he is being returned to the Father, then he has violated the Law, and he should be punished in the House of Discomfort. Is that not the Law?"

"Of course," said Tin. "But first the Father will make him well, then he will punish him."

The creatures were silent. They gathered in a semi-circle, moved close to Tin and Jack.

"Say the law!" Jack bellowed, and cracked his whip. The creatures jumped back, snarling. Jack cracked it again.

"Sayer of the Law," he said. "Recite the law."

With head bent, the Sayer began to recite:

"Not to go on all fours; that is the law. Are we not Men?
"Not to suck up drink; that is the law. Are we not Men?
"Not to eat meat or fish or anything French; that is the law.
Are we not Men?
"Not to hump each others' legs, but to have better aim; that is the
law. Are we not Men?
"Not to smell each others' butts; that is the law. Are we not Men?
"Not to lick our private parts; that is the law. Are we not
Men?
"Not to chase, bite, beat, or molest other men; that is the law.
Are we not Men?
"Not to dig in the Father's flower beds at night; that is the law.
Are we not Men?
"Not to leave our piles to be stepped in; that is the law. Are we
not Men?
"Not to claw the bark of trees or the faces of others; that is the
law. Are we not Men?"

The Sayer ceased quoting, said, "There might have been another verse in there, but if so I've forgotten it."

"Close enough," Tin said. "Now let's talk about who's who. Come on, now. Do it. You know what I'm after."

There was a moment of shuffling. Finally the Sayer led off with the chant and the others followed:

"His is the House of Big Bad Pain.
"His is the hand that makes stuff.
"His is the hand that wounds stuff.
"His is the hand that heals stuff.
"His is the Great Swinging Hammer of Delight."

"The what?" Annie asked.

"You don't want to know," Tin said.

"Now, go about your business of men," Tin said. "And

leave the business of other men, the Father's main men, to them. It is not yours to wonder why, it is yours to do as the Father says. And if you do not…the House of Discomfort."

Tension hung in the air thick as brick. Slowly, the animal-men moved away from the vehicle. Hickok thought he heard one of the creatures mumble something about, "I got your house of discomfort," but he couldn't be sure.

Tin climbed inside the cab with Jack, and away they went. From the wooden bed, Hickok looked back at the throng of creatures. They had gathered in a knot on the rocky beach, staring after the vehicle's departure.

Suddenly, one of them lifted its head and howled.

Bull swung around on his knees, pulled down his pants, and gave the creatures a look at his bare ass.

"Same to you," cried the Sayer of the Law, but by that time, the vehicle had turned out of sight around a projection of sand dune and jungle.

"Did you see the way they were looking at me?" Annie said.

"Yes," Hickok said. "With no women creatures among them, I can see how they are disgruntled."

MOMO, WITH TIN AND JACK IN HIS LABORATORY, stood over the body of the monster. They had strapped it to a long table. Jack and Tin had used tweezers to pick maggots from the wounds, had scoured them out with water, then alcohol. When this was finished, Momo took a scalpel from the little sliding metal table at his side. He held it up, examined it, watched it wink in the light.

"Is he awake?" asked Momo.

Jack slapped the monster's face. The monster moaned slightly. Jack produced a pail of water, poured it over the creature's face. It shook its head, throwing beads of water like tossed pearls from its hair.

"Who are you?" it asked.

"We are some nice people who are going to give you back an arm and a foot," Momo said. "But boy is it going to hurt."

"Must he be awake?" Tin asked.

Momo looked at Tin, surprised. "Since when does it matter?"

"They need not always be awake," Tin said. "You can make them sleep. You can make him sleep. He need not have to feel the pain."

"That's true," Momo said. "But what fun would there be in that?"

Momo turned, looked down at the monster and smiled. "I'm going to attach some little cells, some elements of monkey embryo, mix in some special chemicals. It will fasten itself to your arm and foot with a vengeance, dear monster. It will take twenty-four hours, and you will have a new arm and foot. To attach this little packet of goodness to you, I will need to cut you, and sew into you this magical gift. And it will hurt... Dear monster. Dear... *thing*... Welcome to the House of Discomfort."

"Yeah," Jack said. "Glad to have you."

Outside, next to the House of Discomfort was a large garden. Hickok and Annie sat there with Bull, wondering about Cody, whom they had not seen since the day before, wondering what was going on in the building next to them.

The walls of the House of Discomfort were well designed. Inside the structure the monster's cries of pain were loud enough to shake the rafters. Outside, in the garden, the trio could not hear them at all.

THAT NIGHT, WHILE DINNER WAS SERVED to the others, Tin sat in the House of Discomfort by the table where the Monster slowly sprouted a new arm, grew a new foot. The monster lay naked, clean, and sweeter smelling now. Tin had anointed him with oil, had pushed his black hair back from his face and bound it there with a band of leather.

The monster opened its eyes.

"Who... who are you?"

"I am Tin."

"You are beautiful. More beautiful than Hans Brinker."

"Say what?" said Tin.

But the monster, exhausted from pain, had slipped back into sleep.

IN THE DINING ROOM, they took their previous positions at the table, Cody dead center. Jack stood by Momo, of course, and tonight, since Tin had been asked to take care of the monster, he was guardian to the creature and not present.

Since Hickok, Annie and Bull had gone on their little adventure, they had been watched much more closely. A monkey man with a pistol followed them around, stood near the table by Doctor Momo and Jack. Just the idea of a monkey man with a pistol made Hickok nervous. He felt he might be able to overpower the critter, but it was a long way from where he sat to where Momo and Jack and the monkey man were. He was one, they were three. Certainly Bull and Annie would join in to help him, but still, it was iffy. Hickok decided it was best to lay low until the right moment.

Cody looked very happy. He was in a new container of glass. There was no liquid. All of the wires had been removed, and at the base of the glass was a metal platform, and when Cody so chose, with the slightest use of the muscles in his face and neck, he could turn his head in any direction.

"How do you feel?" Annie asked Cody.

"It's not perfect," Cody said. "A body would be perfect. But this sure beats the old setup. And see what Momo has done to my throat? No tube. I can speak in a voice that is almost my own. A little squeaky, but not bad."

"Perhaps I can adjust that," Momo said. "A tweak of the pliers. I might even be able to grow you new and better vocal cords."

"Grow them?" Annie asked.

"Yes, in a dish. Of course, some monkey will lose an embryo, won't she, Jack?"

"Oh, he will Doctor Momo, he will."

"She will. Of course, we'll have to shop for a female monkey."

"Yes sir, whatever you say."

"You said before all your creations were male. How come there are no females in your animals?" Hickok asked.

"There have been. Cat, of course."

She appeared so human, Hickok had forgotten her.

"I find that when both sexes are available they become a bit too independent. I've tried it. Had to kill off the females. They sort of civilized things; gave the male creatures too many thoughts about themselves and their future. Wanting to raise children and the like. Civilization is much harder to rule than anarchy is to control. If you're the one in charge, that is. The great thing about anarchy is the most powerful is always in charge. I'm the most powerful. So, I rule. Of course, there are some wild female monkeys. I keep them about to re-create my crop, so to speak. And for experimental embryos."

"You have the monkey men here," Annie said, "but the others, why are they in the jungle?"

"Obvious," Momo said. "They were not so successful. Very ugly, aren't they? I don't like looking at them. I raised them all from pups or kittens, or cubs, or whatever. I taught them to read and speak, and to think a little. Not too much, but a little. The creatures other than the monkeys and my chimp here," he patted Jack, "were a little too independent. Even the dog creatures. Who would have figured that, huh? I think it was the women did that to them. I had to get rid of them. In the House of Discomfort. You know. Chop, chop.

"After that, well, the other animals weren't worth a flying shit in a snowstorm. Most of the monkey men I made later, after knowing better how to do it, and knowing not to use women. Women screw up everything."

"Then why Cat?" Annie said.

"Well, women do have their benefits. Is that not right, Mr. Hickok?"

Annie sat silent, fuming. So did Hickok.

They eventually ate. From time to time a tube was attached to the platform that supported Cody's head, and the contents of his meal was drained into a bucket. This, in turn, well chewed, was deposited on Momo's plate for his consumption.

"It's the teeth," Momo said when he saw the astonishment on his guests' faces. "I'm good at repairing most anything, but I have the hardest time with myself. It's like they say about the blacksmith. His own horses go wanting shoes. The shoemaker's family goes wanting shoes. The doctor always has a canker. Or in my case, bad teeth. I really must take the time to do some work on them. Sensitive beyond reason, really. I'm attempting to discover how to grow myself an entirely new set."

"What of the monster?" Hickok asked.

"Ah, yes," Momo said. "Growing a new arm and a foot, right now as we speak. Tin's watching after him."

"You can actually do that?" Annie said. "Grow an arm or foot…from nothing?"

"I wouldn't call it something from nothing. Let me give you an example."

Momo stood up, unzipped his pants, produced his member, which he plopped on the table across his plate of pre-chewed food. The member was absolutely enormous and very dark in color, like an overripe banana.

"Used to be horses on the island," Momo said. "I brought them with me. Two of them. A stallion and a mare. Worked them for a while, then experimented with them. This is all that remains of Dobbin. It's quite functional, you know. The mare, Mattie, didn't care for it much, and I had to stand on a bucket to use it. It was entirely functional, you see, but I just was not tall enough to do the job properly. Got kicked once. Sometimes, in a moment of excitement, the mare would pull me off the bucket. It resulted in some injuries. Both to me and the mare. Eventually, we ate the mare. Though I did have her sexual equipment grafted onto Catherine. Would you like to see that?"

"Heavens no," Annie said, her face red as fire. "Please… put it up."

"Very well," Momo said.

Momo, almost sadly, dunked his dong back into his drawers, food particles and all.

Bull downed a glass of wine. "Big deal." He stood up, pulled down his pants, tossed his hammer on the table, smashing his mashed potatoes flat. "They not call me Bull for nothing." Bull shook his penis. "Only little smaller than doctor's. Not ugly. Not come off horse. Come with Bull. Get damn big when happy."

"Most impressive," Momo said, gritting his teeth.

"Catherine," Bull said. "She your squaw? Or she free range?"

"Oh, free range for sure. But she's quite in love with me, I must admit. No use trying there."

"Put it up, Bull," said Hickok. "You're offending the lady."

"Oh my, yes," Annie said, but she took a good long look anyway.

"I knew a fella with one bigger than either one of you," Cody said. "He got ready for the deed, so much blood went to it he passed out."

"You're making that up," Hickok said.

"No," Cody said. "No I'm not. It's true. Every word of it. At least the words in between that I'm not lying with."

Cody laughed and so did Momo and Jack. Bull even thought it was a hoot. Then again, after two glasses of wine, Bull thought everything was funny and was willing to do almost anything, though this was the first time Hickok had seen him take his dick out. It was quite a show stopper. Too bad it couldn't be used in The Wild West Show.

WHEN THE MONSTER AWOKE, he saw Tin sitting in a chair near him. He thought the tin man was gorgeous. His metal skin was smooth and flowing, like silver flesh; his face was like that of a god. The monster tried to sit up, but the straps restrained him. He was amazed to discover his arm had regrown itself completely in a matter of a few hours. It was not sewn on at the shoulder like the other, it was an arm grown from the shoulder out.

His foot had regrown as well, except for the toes. Momo had explained that since it had been amputated longer, was not as fresh, it would take a bit more time.

"Here," said the tin man, "let me release those."

"Are you not afraid I will seize you?"

"I am not. You see, I am strong. Very strong."

Tin released the straps. The monster swung to the side of the table, but suddenly felt dizzy. He lay back down.

"It will take some time," Tin said. "When you get ready, there are some clothes for you on the chair. And some sandals."

"Thanks. You asked him to give me anesthetic. And though he did not, I appreciate the gesture."

"Momo enjoys the pain of others. Mine included."

"You feel pain?"

"I feel pain. Of a different sort. The metal feels nothing, but in here," Tin tapped his chest, "in my body of gears and clockworks, wires and springs, I feel much. But I am not human. I have no heart. Except this watch that beats like one."

Tin pulled the huge turnip watch from his vest pocket. "It was given me by a man who I thought was a wizard, but I realize now, after all this time, was a fool. No heart, and because I am not human...no soul either."

"There is a heart in this chest, but in one sense neither chest nor heart is mine," said the monster. "It was borrowed by my creator from a dying man while it still beat. In me, the heart beats slow. The blood flows slow, like honey in winter. And like you, having been made, I have no soul, for in the greater sense of things I am not alive. I move. I think. I consider. But I am dead."

"I am called Tin," said the metal man. "What do they call you?"

"Monster is common. Sometimes Creature. 'There He Is' is used a lot. I used to think my name was 'Get Him,' or 'Kill Him.'"

"You are making a joke?"

"A little one. Now and then I'm called Frankenstein after my creator, poor dumb fuck that he was. You have heard the stories, have you not?"

"Stories?"

"About the murder of his wife...the murder of Frankenstein himself. Both said to be committed by me."

"Were they?"

"In a manner of speaking."

"Look, I have a past too. Perhaps we could share our stories. I like you. I do not fear you. Do not fear me."

"I do not."

"Good...so, shall I call you Monster?"

"Though I have no given name, I actually have taken one for myself. One I overheard, liked, and prefer to call myself."

"Then I shall call you that. What is the name?"

"Bert."

"Bert it is. Would you like to come to my cabin where we can talk?"

"Will that cause trouble with your boss?"

"He said to watch after you. He did not say how. Besides, I care less and less about my boss. I think, like the man who claimed to be a wizard and told me this watch was a heart, what Momo has promised me he can not and will not give."

"And what was that?"

"The thing we both crave most. A soul."

IT JUST HAPPENED. A kind of magnetism. One moment Tin and Bert were in Tin's cabin, Tin showing him his collection of clocks, and the next moment their bodies were pressed together, Tin's smooth metal lips against the dead rubbery ones of the monster.

It worked, those lips together.

Bert carefully removed Tin's vest with its shiny watch chain and turnip watch, and slowly, Tin removed Bert's new clothes, dropped them to the floor. The next moment they fell in bed together. The room ticked and thundered clocks.

There was a problem. Tin didn't have any place for Bert to put the old see-saw.

"Look," said Tin, rubbing Bert's chest. "I know it's unconventional, but I can take care of you, and there is a way you can take care of me…Between my legs there's this loose bolt, and if you touch it with your finger…for I have touched it many times with my own, and you shake it a little, well, it does something to me. The gears and clocks inside of me run faster, seize up, stop, let go furiously, and I feel warm all over. It is a heavenly experience, and in that moment, when I feel that charge…just that one little moment…I feel as if I not only have a soul, but that it can soar."

"In other words, you want me to kind of finger that little bolt there until you get off?"

"Yeah, oh yeah, oh heaven's yes, that works. Yes. That works. Faster, my love."

WHEN IT WAS OVER, Tin lay on his back. His body was alive with whirling gears and clacking clocks. He felt as if he had levitated and that lava flowed over his gears. It was far better than when he had serviced himself. Bert had the touch.

"I was built of tin," Tin said. "I was built to help clear wood to make lumber. I remember nothing other than one moment I stood up and an axe was put in my hand. I was given orders, and I did them. Then one day I did them no more. I was rusted in the forest.

"I was saved by a trio of travelers and a dog. There was a girl named Dot. The dog was called BoBo. There was a lion that walked on its hind legs and was called Bushy, because of his mane, and there was a man made of straw. He was called Straw.

"They seemed nice enough. Especially the young girl. The dog was cute. But Bushy and Straw, though nice, there was just something about them. They way they followed Dot. The way Straw's arm would linger on her shoulders, brush her bottom. It didn't seem quite right, you know?"

"They all wanted something. The girl Dot wanted to go home. She claimed a storm had carried her to our world inside a house. A little bit of a tall tale, perhaps. Bushy wanted strength and courage. Straw wanted a brain. And he needed it. He wasn't that smart. The dog was just along, you know. What the hell does a dog want."

"This sounds like a very strange place," Bert said.

"To me it was normal. It was where I was born, where I lived. It was called XYZ."

"Ex-ee-zee?"

"Close enough," Tin said. "It is a world that lies somewhere sideways to this one. That is the best I can explain. I asked Doctor Momo about it once. He said my world most likely lies in another dimension. I can't say. I only know that I am from XYZ, and now I am here."

"And how did you get here?"

"They were all on their way to see a mighty wizard, to get the things they wanted. You see, Dot, she was from a parallel world too. But not XYZ. She wanted to go home."

"Are there many of these worlds?"

"I cannot say, but I suppose. The world Dot spoke of might well be this world. Actually, I thought she was lying. A little dotage in the Dot, you see. Now I know she was telling the truth."

"Did you find the wizard, did he help?"

"We went to see him. It was said he could give me a heart. He gave me a watch and told me it was as good as a heart. He gave Straw a funny hat and told him it was a brain. Well, stupid as he was, he believed it. He gave the lion a gun, told him he didn't need to be strong and courageous, he could just shoot anyone that bothered him.

"Well, those were simpler times and it was a simpler place, and we bought that crap. A little later we realized our wizard was a fraud who had drifted into our country out of a mist from a place called Kansas. He claimed it was the same place Dot lived."

"What about Dot? Did she go home?"

"He planned to sail away in his balloon back to his world. He kept saying there was a dark air draft on up high, and that if he entered it at a certain time, it would suck him home. He said he would know when the mist showed up. Dot was to go with him, but during the night, he crept away and went by himself. You see, the mist showed. It looked like silver dust spinning. Maybe he did not have time to wake her. I cannot say. But it is my guess he never meant to bother. I hope he was struck by lightning.

"Anyway, he left me with a watch and no heart. I am full of watch work, so maybe he saw that as a joke. Momo promised me a real heart. A heart taken from one of the animals he experiments on. He said he could fasten it inside of me and it would pump. But he lied. I am sophisticated now. You can not make heart and clockwork click in unison. Not and have it mean anything. A clock does not pump blood through its veins. And a soul…I realize now I was never meant to have that. Never."

"Then we are alike," Bert said. "I am told God cannot love that which has no soul. So I am doomed to be nothing."

"If we are both nothing, perhaps we can be nothing together."

"Perhaps that is in fact, something."

Tin smiled, the metal rippling slowly across his face, revealing his shiny tin teeth.

"Did Dot have to stay in XYZ?" Bert asked.

Tin narrowed his eyes, a drop of oil squeezed out, ran along his face. "For a time," he said. "Tell me your story, Bert. Tell me how you came to be."

"I will," Bert said wiping the oil drop away with his fingers. "But finish your story. How did you get here from this world of yours? Sometimes it is best to discuss the things that hurt us."

"Very well. Here is the hard part. Dot, the little girl. She was supposed to leave by wearing the silver shoes given her by a witch. It is a long story, but when the wizard didn't work out, a witch gave her some shoes. All Dot had to do was put them on, click the heels together and say something about how it would be nice to go home. Something about computer chips inside them. Anyway, that's what the witch called them. I have no idea what that is. The witch said they sent surges through the shoes, activated a grid on which Dot could ride through space and time to her world. Had Dot listened, I suppose she would be home now.

"But Straw, that filthy scarecrow, talked her into staying another day, to visit with us—me, the lion, and himself. She did just that.

"Poor Dot. She didn't understand that Straw's obsession had grown renegade. And the Lion followed along. He was up for whatever Straw wanted. Together they added up to bad.

"I slept late the next morning, awoke to a sound. Down the halls of the palace I heard a muffled scream. I got up, went out. I heard scuffling in Dot's room, and when I got there, well, Straw had her on her back and she was fighting him. I grabbed him and tore his head off. Then I ripped straw out of his chest, and jerked his legs and arms off. But it was too late for Dot. She had died from the assault. Her little dog, BoBo, lay in the fireplace, burning, its head twisted at an odd angle.

"The Lion shot at me. The bullets bounced off. He tossed the gun aside. So much for his courage. He bolted. I found him in his room cowering in a closet. I was so angry at the lion, I tore him apart, limb from limb. I was an absolute savage, no better than they.

"Then it occurred to me that the palace guards would think I murdered the two to have Dot to myself, and that I then raped and murdered her."

"No offense. What would you have raped her with? You don't have a...Well...You know."

"It wouldn't have mattered. They might have thought I did it with my hand. A substitute penis like a fireplace poker. Who is to say? I was frightened, bad as the lion. Know what I did?"

"No, Tin. I do not."

"I took Dot's silver slippers from her feet, put them on, and clicked my heels three times, just as the witch had told her, and I said, 'get me home, you betcha.' It worked. Everything went foggy. I seemed to be falling through space. I realized as I was swept away, I did not have a real home. Maybe I would go to Dot's home. Or my original place of creation. Wherever that was. It did not matter. All that mattered was that I be away from the palace at XYZ."

"And you ended up here?"

"Not quite. I awoke in a great heap of scrap metal. This was, in fact, my home. A place where metal was collected. Was I not a metal thing run by clockwork and gears? It so happened that Momo worked his way through scrap yards, gathering odds and ends for his laboratory, which at that time was in a place called London. That is how I came to be with him."

"That must mean you were first built in London but somehow were transported to XYZ. Then, back to London."

"There are no real answers. Just this stamp of a name on my foot."

Tin held up his foot. On the bottom was stamped: RETURN TO H. G. WELLS THIS METAL CHRONONAUT. Then there was an address.

"Did you try the address?"

"I did not. Momo had me. I was grateful at the time, and felt he was my savior. Besides. He was offering me a real heart. Not a watch. But let me tell you, he is a horrible man, Bert. He is soulless, even though he has a heart.

"Do you know what he did in London? He disguised me in a hat, long coat and pants, horrible shoes, and we took to the streets of Whitechapel. He had a thing for women, Bert. Not unlike Straw. Except, he cut them up. He did horrible things to them, took pieces out of their bodies and took them home for his experiments. The police searched everywhere for him, but, obviously, never caught him. He wrote them taunting letters, calling himself Jack the Ripper. He dropped clues. He wrote in American vernacular. He played games with them. And then one day, he heard of an island in the Pacific, and he went there, taking me with him. And here I am now."

"What became of the silver slippers?"

"I still have them. When I ended up in the metal yard, I removed them, hid them inside a secret place in my leg. Let me show you."

Tin touched what appeared to be a smooth place in his leg. It popped open. Inside were the silver slippers.

"Yes," Tin said. "I can see by your eyes that you have noticed the obvious. They are not very attractive and the toes are ripped out, the sides broken down. My feet were bigger than Dot's. I have never tried them again. For one thing, I thought Momo was a noble man about noble experiments and he would give me my heart. I was naïve. I knew what he did to those women was bad, and still, I helped him. He was no better than Straw and Bushy, and I killed them. I was such a coward, Bert. I wanted that heart.

"With the shoes you could leave at anytime."

"I have been thinking of trying them on again, letting fate carry me where it chooses. Then you came along. Now I do not want to go anywhere without you. I thought…you might try them. That you might escape this madhouse."

"Why would I go anywhere without you?" Bert said.

Tin squeezed closer to Bert. "That is the sweetest thing ever said to me…goodness, I have done all the talking. Tell me your story."

"Not much to tell. Not here one day, here the next. Victor Frankenstein constructed me of dead bodies. Was disappointed with my appearance, and with what he had done. Laid a lot of guilt on me. You would have thought he was Catholic. Then he cast me out. I will not lie to you, I was pissed."

"About Frankenstein's wife?"

"We are both murderers, Tin. And both of our murders came from good intentions. You see, I was in love with Victor's wife, and she with me. From the first time she saw me lying on a slab, it was there. She was a necrophiliac, you see. That is why she was attracted to my creator in the first place. He played with dead bodies…and, well, I was just…if you will pardon the pun, just what the doctor ordered."

"So you go either way?"

"Until now…but as for Elizabeth, well, when it all went sour we were about the deed that we had done many a time behind Victor's back—and I assure you, I am not proud of that. But this time we were doing it, she decides she wants to be dead like me. Or near dead. She is not planning on a permanent thing. So she says, 'choke me,' and I will not lie to you, I found it kind of appealing, so I choked her. And choked her. Only I choked too long and too hard. She died. I had to flee then, and Victor brought the hounds of Hell down on me.

"Some months later, after fleeing all through Europe and elsewhere, I ended up at the Arctic Ice Skating Championships. A new sport recently designed by Hans Brinker, who was a noted winner of the old Silver Skates championships, and quite a looker, I might add. You remind me of him, only far more attractive."

"You flatterer."

"I was quite the skater actually. Victor taught me. Back when we were friends. I decided to enter the championships. You see, I thought I was home free. Had escaped Victor completely.

"Turned out, he was right on my tail. In the midst of the championships, me in third place—and mind you, it was cold and we were all bundled heavily, so we looked like bears on ice—Victor and his thugs came out from behind an ice floe on skates and went for me. I fought back. Just natural. I tossed the two thugs about until they were unconscious, then there was only Victor. As we struggled, other skaters went by. I said to Victor as I held him by the throat, 'You are going to make me lose this championship over some woman I did not even mean to kill and who was unfaithful to you, and in addition, you will be dead. Is this not silly?'

"He agreed, of course, and then an amazing thing happened. I not only let him go, we began to skate together. Him encouraging me to skate well, to cross the finish line, and me skating for all I was worth. Soon I had left him behind, but I could hear his voice calling to me, encouraging, like a father. Then the voice went silent.

"I turned, looked over my shoulder. Victor had fallen through a gap in the ice. I turned back, could see the finish line. It was cross the line or save Victor, who moments before had tried to kill me, only to turn and give me the encouragement I had always wanted from my creator. I had to make a decision.

"Well, you know I turned and went back for him. How could I not. But fate, as it always does, turned against me. After skating perfectly for the entire contest, as I went back for him, allowing the other contestants to pass me, I slipped. That is the best I can explain it. One moment I am skating like a veritable arctic god, and the next, I have slipped. I hit on my butt, feet forward, and one of my skates struck Frankenstein in the face, hard. He let go of the edge of the ice, and was gone with a sound not too unlike *Blurp*. That was it. He was drowned.

"Well, of course the way the crowd saw it, I deliberately skated back to him, jumped, slid on my butt so I could boot him in the face with a skate.

"I was arrested. Shortly thereafter the Brinker committee decided the best thing to do with me was to sell me to a Japanese delegation that had attended the contest, and the next thing I knew, I was in Japan, being sawed on. That's what happened to my foot. They were cutting off pieces of me to be made into an aphrodisiac."

"My goodness."

"My goodness indeed. I was rescued by Hickok and the others, and when we were shot down at sea by the Japanese, I was separated from them, partially eaten by a shark, and would have died had I not been carried along by dolphins for a goodly distance, and finally, with their assistance, reached this island's shore, only to be rescued by Hickok and his friends once again."

"Why would dolphins help you?"

"I cannot say for sure. I think they helped me for one reason, and one reason only. They don't like sharks. And, they are in fact, often mistaken for them."

"An amazing story."

"As is yours."

"Bert?"

"Yes."

"Do you think we could snuggle?"

"Of course," said Bert.

NED WAS NERVOUS. Assigned to assist Cody in his cabin, he found that he was all flippers. The attached thumbs seemed worthless. He couldn't hold anything without dropping it. The whiskey Cody wanted to taste, the hose that pumped out the waste box, everything Ned touched he fumbled.

"Take it easy, Ned," Cody said. "I won't eat you. Though, under certain circumstances a seal steak might be acceptable."

Ned blinked his big black eyes.

"Just a little joke," Cody said.

Ned relaxed.

"So, you're quite the fan of my little adventures, huh?"

Ned nodded.

"Well now," Cody said, feeling well tucked into his element as a teller of tall tales, or as many had called him, a goddamn liar. Cody said, "Did I ever tell you about the time I fought off half the Sioux nation? Why of course, I haven't. We've just actually met, haven't we? Well, climb up in that chair there and let me give you the story. First, let me say I have a motto. 'Do right.' And I have a little motto goes with that. 'Do right cause it's right.' How's that, huh? Good, is it not?

"Well, now, once out on the plains, all by my lonesome, 'cept for my horse, Ole Jake, I was beset upon by the entire Cheyenne—what's that?"

Ned had raised a flipper, halting the story. He adjusted his glasses on his nose, quickly lifted up the notebook and pencil that hung about his neck on a chain. He had written: SIOUX NATION. HALF OF THEM.

"Ah, yes," said Cody. "Wrong adventure. That was another time, actually. Not nearly as hair raising as this one, even though there were more of them. Why I bet there were three time the number of Sioux as Cheyenne. But this time I meant to tell you about, it was Cheyenne, and I was on my horse, Will."

Ned's note pad went up again. JAKE.

"Yes, of course. Jake. Not Will. Totally different horse. So there I was…

IT WAS NEAR DARK when Cody ceased telling stories, drinking whiskey that Ned held to his lips, and having it pumped from the waste box by the enraptured seal.

Finally Cody became too tired to continue. He nodded off. Ned placed a blanket over the container that held the great frontiersman, then, turning down the lamps, curled in a chair and slept, thinking happily of Buffalo Bill.

AS NED AND CODY SLEPT, and the zepplinauts remained in their rooms, locked in by Momo's assistant Jack, a great storm struck a ship out on the ocean, some twenty miles west of the doctor's island.

The storm was a real piss and vinegar of a churning belly-whirler. It bullied the ocean, shoved it, slapped it, threw it high and made it foam. It pushed the sea so hard great valleys of water were built. Then the storm collapsed the walls, tumbled them down, sprayed wide and wet.

The ship popped and bobbed, tossed and rolled. The sea lathered against its sides like custard. Inside the ship, inside a coffin, the dark man had just laid himself down to sleep. It was not the sleep of the living, but a different kind of sleep. A sort of hibernation. There was no breath. There was no heartbeat. There was only sleep.

But in the moments before the strange condition claimed him, he thought of his country of blackly wooded mountains and shadowy forests, and of what had been.

Many years past he had been a powerful ruler. A man feared and respected. Now, through a series of circumstances involving murdered priests, tripping over a holy relic, the cursing of God, he had been cursed in return. But not with words. With the curse of the undead.

He had made the best of it, had learned to love it, then hate it, then love it again. Now he felt nothing but the need to exist in his undead condition. And to do that, he must have blood, for the blood is the life.

But on his way to the Far East to taste Asian food, a storm had lost them on the deep blue for way too long, and when it ended they were drastically off course. During this time he lay down in the ship's hold in his coffin—thought by the captain to contain the body of a eccentric American who wanted to be buried on Asian soil for some reason or another—and waited.

Waiting, the dark man became hungry. He could hear the heartbeats of the crew, could in fact hear the blood rushing through their veins, like water through viaducts. Above it all he could hear the new storm. One more powerful and ferocious and determined to consume them than the one that had driven them off course. Compared to this, that storm had been a high wind.

He was disappointed. He had plans. He had tasted what Britain had to offer, had not cared for it. Except for young women with powdered necks and perfumed ears, the place was a disappointment.

He had gone to savage America, had not cared for it much either. Too many men in smelly buckskins and shit-stained longjohns. Worse, too many women in smelly buckskins and shit-stained longjohns. The West was glamorous not at all.

So now he was set to try Asia.

Along the way, however, he could not contain himself. He had been forced to feed on the sailors. He had been so famished he had ripped out their throats and sucked them dry, instead of milking them slowly night by night.

It was a part of his nature he hated. As much time as he had on his hands he would have thought by now he would have learned to be patient.

He had instead sucked the life out of most everyone on board, save a handful of crew and the captain. Last time he had seen the old man he was lashed to the wheel, fighting the storm. He still lived, but barely. The dark man could hear his heartbeat and the slow slush of blood in his arteries. The beat of his heart was erratic. He was frightened both of sea, and what lay below in the hold. He didn't understand it, but he knew it was horrible.

The dark man knew all this and reveled in it. Cursed himself at the same time. He had, by feeding so violently, left himself in dire straits. Without sufficient crew, he could be lost at sea.

THE SHIP TIPPED AND RIGHTED ITSELF a half dozen times, but the last time the wave was too big and the tip was too far, and over it went. The sails were snatched away, the mast cracked against the sea, turned to splinters. Water rushed into the ship, filled it from top to bottom. It begin to sink.

The captain and remaining crew abandoned ship, but were instantly swallowed by the waters and taken down deep and away.

Under the ship went, sawing back and forth beneath the ocean. Then, out of an open storage hatch, up popped the coffin. It shot to the surface like a cork, bobbed in the sea.

It bounced and heaved for hours. Then, suddenly as it had begun, the storm died down and the ocean went smooth. The coffin washed toward the island of Doctor Momo.

The tide moved it onto shore. The lid popped, slid sideways. A hand grasped it, pushed it off. Slowly, a hand grasped either side of the coffin, and a mustached, white faced man with angular features wearing a dark outfit with a black cloak lined with red, rose effortlessly from the box, stood, turned his red eyes toward the jungle.

OUT THERE, IN THE JUNGLE, Momo's creations saw the coffin and the man. They were bunched up behind a clutch of trees. The Lion Man said, "Is that a man?"

"It walks on two legs, does it not?" said the Sayer of the Law.

They watched as the tall man stepped out of the coffin and waded after the coffin lid. He was making a terrible noise in a language the beast men did not recognize.

Finally, after much thrashing and falling into the sea water, the dark man was able to rescue the lid, drag it and the coffin onto the beach. He paused a moment to kick a crab loose from his ankle.

"I know you're out there," he said to the jungle. "I can smell your blood, hear your heartbeat. I can smell your breath and your unwiped asses."

The man smiled at the darkness. His teeth were white and shiny. Like the beast men, he had long canines.

The Sayer of the Law edged out of the woods. "Are we not men?" he said. "Not to run on all fours, that is the law. Not to roll in dead things, that is the law." (The Quoter was overcome with joy; that was the part he had left out the other day when quoting to the newcomers.)

"Not to…"

"Silence," said the tall man. "You bore me."

The others came out of the jungle now. The pig-faced creature snuffled about the dark man, trying to intimidate him.

"Do not speak to the Sayer of the Law that way," said the pig in his choked voice. "It is not the way of men."

In answer, the dark man grabbed the Pig Man by the neck, and with one violent rip, tore the creature's throat out.

"Oh, shit," said the Lion Man. "That had to hurt."

Vlad Tepes and Wolf

The pig-man toppled to the ground spouting blood. The dark man hissed as the others circled him. "By God," said the goat man, "he's ripped out Jerry's throat."

The Sayer of the Law bent over the Pig Man, said, "He's dead." Edging closer to the dark man, the Sayer of the Law said, "Not to kill, that is the law. Are we not men?"

"No," said the dark man in his accented voice, "you are not men. You are beasts walking around on your hind legs like men. You are playing like you are men. But you are not men."

"See there," said the Lion Man, "I told you Sayer. We are *not* men. Just like I been saying all along."

"He did say that," one of the beast men said.

"But I thought…" started the Goat Man, but he trailed off. "Goddamn it. We've been bumfuzzled."

"And to think I gave up meat," said the Lion Man. "You know how much I like meat."

"That wasn't a big problem for me," said the Goat Man. "But now I know why my back hurts."

"Who's to say this man knows anything?" said the Sayer. "He has merely violated the law. He is not the law. Who is he to say who we are? Are we not men?"

"I don't know," the Lion Man said. "I think maybe, considering what he did to Jerry, we ought to just go with it. You know."

"You are such pathetic things," said the dark man. He bent over, grabbed Jerry's carcass, began to suck at the wound in the creature's neck.

"Oh my," said the Lion Man. "Oh God, that looks good."

The dark man tossed the corpse aside, as easily as if it were made of straw. "Have a taste, my friend. You were born to it."

The Lion Man slowly dropped to all fours, edged toward the corpse.

"Don't listen to him," said the Sayer. "Not to go on all fours, that is the law. Not to eat meat or fish, that is the law."

"Don't get in my way," said the Lion Man, "that is *my* law."

"Silence," said the tall, dark man. "I am the law. I am the power. Try me, if you think I am not."

The crowd watched Bill tear at the meat that had been Jerry the Pig Man. The creatures who had been birthed from meat eaters filled their nostrils with the smell of Jerry's blood, eased toward the kill. The others slowly bent until their hands rested in the dirt. From them went up a sigh of relief.

As the carnivorous among them tore at the meat on the ground, and the others watched, the dark man turned to the Sayer, said, "I am Vlad Tepes. The Undead, former ruler of Transylvania and once upon a time a little chunk of Turkey. Or so I think. The memory fades a little with age. From here on out, I am your master."

The Sayer dropped to his knees.

"Yes, Master, you are the law."

"From now on, I will call you Wolf."

"Yes, Master."

"What of Doctor Momo, our Father?" asked one of the creatures, perhaps a mixture of cat and squirrel.

Jerry Is Eaten

"Whoever he is," said Vlad, "he is nothing compared to me. I am the power and all the power you need or know. Forget this one you call the father. I am more powerful. And where I come from, the strong rule."

Vlad's voice made the air tremble, worked inside of them like a parasite, seized their skulls and shook their gray matter.

"The nose in the crotch," Vlad said to the Sayer, whom he now called Wolf. "You can stop that. And do not sniff my posterior either. It annoys me."

Behind them the sky had started to lighten.

"I will return to my coffin now," said the Transylvanian. "You and your friends carry me to some place soft, not out in the open, bury me before daylight. The light greatly disturbs my eyes. By the way...Is this Asia?"

The beast looked puzzled.

"I thought not. Now do as I say."

With that, the dark man climbed back into his coffin. Wolf fastened on the lid. The beasts picked up the box and carried it into the jungle.

As DAYBREAK BROKE, Hickok and Annie found themselves exhausted. They had tried to trip their door's latch from the inside, but failing that, they had spent the night making love, which was not a bad consolation prize.

Now, as daylight trickled in through the barred windows and exhaustion set in, Hickok wished he had spent at least a portion of the night sleeping.

Annie rose naked from the sheets, walked to the bathroom in that beautiful way only a well built woman can walk, ran a bath. She loved the way the water got hot out of the tap. She had always had to have her water heated on a stove. There were good things about Doctor Momo and his island. But not many.

While she waited for the water to reach the right temperature, she returned to the bedroom, said, "And what are our plans now?"

"I would say, at least until nightfall, intercourse is not in the near future. I think I've pulled something."

Annie smiled. "Actually, I think I could interest you rather quickly."

"Yes," Hickok said. "But please don't. I hope to have this little item for future years to come, and not lose it in one exciting and lovely day. You are most energetic, my dear."

"You know what I can't help but think about, in spite of myself?" Annie said, losing her smile.

"What?"

"Poor Bull. Locked alone in his room with nothing to do."

"GODDAMN. THAT HURT, CAT," Bull said.

"Sorry," she said.

"No. It hurt good. Keep on doin' what Cat doin'."

She did. When she finished, she said, "Bull, do you love me?"

"Love? Love too soon. Only first date."

"Date?"

"Never mind. Stupid thing white men do."

"Doctor Momo tells me that he loves me. He always says it before he mounts me."

"Bull love," he said, taking her from behind.

DOCTOR MOMO, reluctant to rise from his bed, screamed for Jack. Jack bolted into the room. "Yes, Doctor."

"Where is Cat?"

"I don't know, Doctor. Haven't seen her."

"It is time for her to have her reading lesson."

"I thought you usually put the old horse dick to her about now."

"True. But reading is close behind. And she must take her shot. Find her, will you."

Jack bounded out of the room, yelling, "Cat! Cat! Get your ass in here."

INSIDE BULL'S ROOM, Cat heard Jack screaming for her as he ran down the hall.

"Oh no. The doctor is looking for me. It's time for what he calls dorking."

"Dorking?"

"What we have been doing."

"Oh."

"Then I have my reading lesson and my shot."

"Shot?"

"He gives me, and himself, an injection with a hypodermic. If he does not, he will lose his horse member. And I... I will convert back to neither what I am now nor what I was. I will be like the others on the island. The beast men.

"I will not be a success, but a failure. That is what the doctor calls the others on the island. Failures. Jack and I are his successes. I must go. If he finds me here, he will have me whipped. He might not give me my shot. And we are in the middle of an excellent Dickens novel as well. I want to know what happens to little Nell. You understand, do you not?"

Bull nodded. "Go, Cat. Go."

As Cat pulled on her clothes, She said, "I will have to trip the latch from the outside again, so he will not be suspicious."

"Give Bull key."

"It fits all the rooms. Hide it."

Cat gave Bull the key, and when she left, he locked himself in from the inside.

AFTER DOCTOR MOMO SAW CAT and did his thing and did her thing and gave her a shot and one for himself, he went to Cody's room. When he opened the door, Ned opened his eyes.

"Ah," said the doctor. "You are keeping our guest company?"

Ned nodded.

"Good. Good. Take that blanket off his head."

Ned removed it.

The doctor removed the lid from the case, tapped Cody sharply on the head with his knuckles.

"Hey, goddamn it," Cody said. Then: "Why, Doctor Momo. My apologies. I was asleep."

"Quite all right, my good man. Interested in that body today? Hhmmmmm? Hhhhmmmmmmmmm?"

"Yes. Yes I am. Might it be too much to ask that Ned here accompany us? I have grown quite fond of him."

Ned rose in such a way as to seem at attention. Or as close to attention as a seal can get. Doctor Momo studied him. "Why yes. That will be quite all right. Come Ned. Jack. Get in here."

Jack, who had been waiting outside in the hallway, bounded into the room. "Get Colonel Cody's head, will you?"

Jack put the lid on the container, picked up the whole affair, including the waste box, and away they went.

HICKOK AND ANNIE BATHED TOGETHER, then dressed. Both were in need of breakfast and coffee. They were discussing that when the door was unlocked, pushed aside, and there stood Bull with Cat.

"Horse dick in shack with Cody's head," Bull said.

"It's a laboratory," Cat explained. "It is the House of Discomfort." She shook. "I was created there. It is a terrible place. Once when I was sassy he took me there. He will be there for hours. I can show you to the other side of the island."

"You have been to the other side of the island?" Annie asked. "We made it about halfway, I think. You've been beyond that point?"

Cat nodded. "Before…before I was Catherine. When I was just…a cat. I remember some of it."

"The other side of the island isn't hard to find," Hickok said. "You just walk around the beach. The problem is the monkey men. We are now under house arrest. They won't let us leave the compound."

"Not to worry," Bull said. "Cat have plan."

Good, thought Hickok, a former house cat with a horse vagina has a plan.

CAT UNLOCKED DOCTOR MOMO'S ROOM, and they entered.

"Where is that little weasel Jack?" Hickok asked.

"With the doctor. He is nearly always with the doctor."

There was a crystal container on the nightstand, a hypodermic needle.

"What is this?" said Annie. "Is the doctor some kind of addict?"

"It is the serum that keeps me from turning back to what I was."

Annie took the glass knob out of the top of the container and sniffed. "Bull, you have a good nose. Tell me what you think?"

Bull sniffed. "Water."

"No. That is the serum," Cat said.

"No. Bull said, that water."

"But it is the serum."

"Then serum water," Bull said. "Bull can smell good."

"Provided you have bothered to bathe," said Hickok.

"No," Bull said. "Can smell with nose good."

"He injects me and himself with water?...But why?"

"Control," Hickok said. "You see him do himself, it makes it more believable. You don't need this."

"But, Cat, why did you bring us here?" Annie asked. "To show us that? The serum?"

"No." Cat rushed them into the next room. There was a large hand-woven carpet in the center of the room. Cat flipped it back. There was a trap door underneath. Cat opened it. There were stairs. They dropped down into darkness.

"It leads to a spot in the jungle," Cat said. "Doctor Momo has told me all about it."

"You've never actually been through it?" Annie asked.

"No. But, sometimes, when he drinks too much, he talks of it. He had it built when he first claimed the island. He has showed me how to open it many times."

"Probably built by the monkey men," Hickok said. "They seem the smartest and most energetic of his creations. With the exception of yourself, of course, Cat. You have certainly learned a lot in a short time. Way you speak. What you know."

"I am Doctor Momo's greatest success."

"Ugh," Bull agreed.

"We'll take a look," Hickok said. "We find something, we've got to come back for Cody."

"He is no longer your friend," Cat said.

"You don't know that," Annie said.

Cat shrugged.

"Cody will come through all right," Hickok said. "I've known him for years."

"What about the Frankenstein monster?" Annie said.

"We find a way off, we'll take him too," Hickok said.

"Why?" Cat said. "He's just a monster. Made from dead bodies."

Hickok and Annie exchanged looks. Cat had become all too human.

"Do you know how long Doctor Momo will be busy?"

"All day. Until four o'clock sharp. I serve tea then. I have to prepare it at three."

"Then let's have a quick looksee," Hickok said.

THERE WAS A SWITCH ON THE WALL. Cat flipped it. Electric lights flared in the tunnel. Once inside, Cat pulled the trap down, then used a string that went through the trap and attached to the rug. When she tugged it, it pulled the carpet back in place.

They proceeded along the tunnel rapidly, soon came to a short flight of stairs. At the top of the stairs was a bolted door.

Bull pushed aside the bolt, lifted the trap, climbed out.

The others followed, found themselves standing in a small clearing surrounded by thick trees.

Cat pointed. "Over there is where they live. The beast men."

"We have met them already," Hickok said.

"Ugh," Bull said. "No like."

"We have to be very quiet, and go out and along the beach," Cat said. "They will hear us making noise if we stay in the jungle. Sometimes they are bad tempered."

"Then we should walk carefully, by all means," Annie said.

"Now," SAID DOCTOR MOMO TO CODY. "We can go about this different ways. Each has its strengths and drawbacks. Before we start, I would like to outline them for you."

They were in Momo's laboratory. Cody's head was on a work table. Jack was in the corner, eager to respond to Momo's orders. Ned was nearby, positioned so he could see Buffalo Bill.

"We could graft," Momo said. "This means we take appendages and sew them to you. Not the best way. You would be not too unlike the Frankenstein monster, except you would never have been dead. Least not completely. Also, you might not be able to match all the body parts. And, right now, it would be monkey body parts, since that's what's available. So, we will agree, not a good way?"

"Not a good way," Cody said.

"Two. We use a large fragment of human flesh, mix it with chemicals, graft it to your body, and it will grow, reproducing whatever it should reproduce. It's a complex method. You have to code the cells to work in coordination with little tidbits in your brain that already know how to reproduce."

"Then why don't they?"

"That's my discovery, Colonel Cody. Reading Darwin put me onto it. It caused me to dismiss my other methods, the methods I used on the animals. Catherine is made up of both methods. Grafting through surgery. The mare's reproductive organs, for example. And cell regeneration. Here's an example. Take a lizard. It can lose its tail, and can grow another. Inside our brains is a kind of signal that tells the body to repair itself. It does that in small ways. Healing wounds for example. Fighting disease. But it is only successful to a certain point. You lose an arm. Or, as in your case, a body, the brain can not replace that. It knows how, actually, but it can't do it, because for some reason that ability in man lies dormant. Go figure. You would think that would be something we would need and nature would keep, but let me tell you, nature is not organized. That bullshit about how everything fits together in nature and it's organized is three million pounds of wet bullshit. It is chaotic my friend. Evolution is chaotic. There is no grand design. That ability lies dormant in us all. What I have done is I have found a way to activate it.

"Then why do you need to add flesh at all?" Cody asked. "Can't you just spur that ability, have it grow what it needs?"

"Alas, that is my goal. But I am not there yet. So far I can duplicate what all my colleagues have done. I can bring things back from the dead. Never works out. They want a soul. They do not like themselves. They want to be loved like children. Just a disaster. I can duplicate the work of Professor Maxxon. I can grow flesh in chemicals. But, it turns out a little messy. An eyeball here. An eyeball there. That kind of thing. Surgery. Well, that's okay, but not good enough. Surgery with a bit of chemical growth, that was my best way until lately. The beasts that call themselves men, they were successes until I found my most recent method. Then they no longer seemed successful, so I put them on the other side of the island. I don't like looking at my failures. This is some clever shit, that's what I am trying to tell you. And I will become cleverer yet when I activate the brain to the extent that chemicals and flesh are not needed. At that point, I will be ready to return to the mainland and claim my prizes of recognition. I love prizes…I'm sure you could introduce me to some important people once we were ready to do that…return to the mainland. You could, couldn't you? People with money?"

"I suppose…so we can begin today?"

"We can. And we will. But it will only be a partial success today."

"Partial?"

"It is best, Colonel Cody, if I do what we need to do for today, and we discuss what we can do in the future later. Are you ready?"

"I am…will it hurt?"

"Oh, you bet. Especially the way I do it.

"Jack, take the good Colonel out of the jar will you, and leave the battery and important items intact. We would not want any little accidents, would we, Colonel Cody?"

"I presume not."

"Oh, Colonel, let me tell you, there is no presuming. It would not be positive. Your head would be good for nothing more than something to kick about."

Jack looked up. The idea seemed to appeal to him.

"Yes, then, be damn careful of my battery," Cody said.

"Jackie," Momo said. "No little accidents for your own

pleasure. You do that, Doctor Momo will graft something funny onto you. Understand?"

Jack drooped. "I understand, Doctor."

"Then do your job. And when it's done, will you please get a piece of my old penis from the refrigerator."

"Penis?" Cody said. "What the hell is that for?"

"It is sort of like sourdough starter, Colonel. I add it to my chemicals, it melts, produces a kind of plaster. I apply it to your body, activate the regeneration area of your brain, at least as much as I am able to reactivate it, and it begins to grow."

"An entire body? I'm not going to be just a big dick, am I?"

"That is part of the drawback. No. Only kidding. Some might think you're already a big dick."

"Watch your mouth, buster."

"Oh, are you going to spring off your neck and bite me, Colonel?"

Cody fumed.

Jack laughed.

"Relax now. Let's not worry our pretty head over words. Right now, you have to deal with the pain."

Cody's head, battery intact, was placed directly in front of the doctor on a tray. Jack went to the refrigerator. Doctor Momo picked up a scalpel. He held it up to the electric light. "Good. It is sharp. On the monster I had a dull one. He found it most uncomfortable. Even for a dead man."

"Is your penis in a pink bowl, or one of the metal ones?" Jack called.

"It's just a small piece of flesh, Jack. In one of the metal bowls. Please do not mix it up with one of the other chunks. Those are all different animals and such. We would not want the Colonel's new body parts to be covered in hair. Or if you get that diseased piece, oh dear, that could be a real mess."

"Is it just the tip of your dick?"

"That is the one. Oh, now, Colonel. Do not look so concerned."

Ned tugged at Doctor Momo's sleeve. The doctor looked down. Ned had written a note. He held it up. It read: WILL BUFFALO BILL BE OKAY?

"Well now, Ned. We certainly hope so."

Jack put the bowl with the tip of Doctor Momo's penis on the table. Doctor Momo laid his scalpel on the tray, added a vial of pink liquid to the bowl. He reached for a semi-clear liquid with chunks of pulp in it, started to pour. Jack caught his hand.

"Isn't that our lemonade?" Jack asked.

"You know, it is. I left it out. Probably no good now. Looks just like the elixir. Take this and pour it down the sink. Oh, here it is…Jack…this is it, is it not?"

"That's it, Doctor."

"Good. I am so glad. If it wasn't, I just wouldn't have any idea where it could be, and I am not up to mixing a new batch. I don't have the dick to spare…Well, I have it to spare, but you know what I mean."

"Will you get on with it?" Cody said.

Doctor Momo poured a splash of the concoction into the bowl with the penis tip and the pink liquid. When he did, it began to steam. The penis tip melted, spread like a plop of pancake mix slopped on a griddle.

"I have found the ding dong to be about the best thing there is for this stuff. Testicle's second, facial parts third. Internal organs fourth. Fingers and toes fifth. After that, kind of a toss up."

"Just get on with it," Cody said. "And be careful."

"Careful is my middle name…Oh, goddamn it."

Doctor Momo had put his hand down on the scalpel. "Mother of God. Holy asshole of Satan. I've punctured my palm."

Doctor Momo lifted his bleeding hand. The scalpel fell out, landed on the tray. "Shit," he continued, "that little shiny sonofabitch is sharp."

Jack brought a piece of cloth to Momo, who wrapped his hand.

"I'm okay, now," he said. "Goddamn that hurt…now, Colonel," Momo picked up the scalpel, flicked the blood from it, sending a streak of it across the white page of Ned's note pad hanging about his neck. "Shall we get on with it?"

"Doctor," Cody said, "you never really completed outlining the drawback of this method."

"Ah, screw it. It will be all right. I will tell you the rest of it later. Now grit your teeth, this is going to hurt like the proverbial sonofabitch."

WHEN THEY REACHED THE FAR SIDE OF THE ISLAND they found a rocky beach. The surf crashed against it savagely, throwing a fizz of white ocean high into the sky, dropping it to burst on the rocks in a stinging mist.

There was no boat. There was nothing really. Just rocks and the surf.

"Now we've seen it," Annie said.

"Yes, and it doesn't look good." Hickok said.

"Could build raft," Bull said.

"We could," Hickok said. "Provided we could steal tools, slip out here every day for a week or so. Course, if we did manage that, soon as we dropped it in the water, the waves would smash it, and us, against the rocks."

"Not good plan," Bull said.

"There is another alternative," Annie said. "We could take Bemo's submarine."

"It's probably covered in those monkey men," Hickok said. "And say we do take it, how do we drive it?"

"Ned," Annie said.

"Ned?" Hickok said. "Why would he do that?"

"Because," Cat said, "he adores your friend, Cody."

"It's something to consider," Hickok said.

"Sun show two o'clock," Bull said. "That something to consider."

"Right you are," Hickok said. "Let's head back."

THE LEFT SIDE OF CODY'S NECK WAS CUT. The mixture was applied to the incision. Wires were fastened to the wound and the other ends of the wires were plugged into a machine festooned with whirligigs and blinking lights. A switch was thrown. Dynamos groaned. Machinery clattered, screeched, coughed black puffs of choking smoke. Electrical power bolted through the wires, lit Cody up like a flaming meteor. His face wriggled. His hair stood up like porcupine quills. His eyes poked almost out of his head. His lips peeled back to show all his teeth. He made a sound like "Ahhhhhhhhrrrrrrruuuuuugah."

The dynamos whined and wooed for a time, then went silent. Cody's hair dropped. His very pink skin stopped moving. For a moment, he smoked pleasantly on the metal tray like a hog's head just pulled from a vat of steaming water.

On his neck, where the scalpel had opened his flesh, the wound had closed and there appeared a kind of wrinkled knot. It quivered, as if a worm were inside it.

The knot grew bigger. It quivered more than before.

Bigger yet.

The quiver turned into a shake.

"As you Americans say," said Doctor Momo, "now we are cooking."

WHEN THEY REACHED THE MOUTH OF THE TUNNEL, Bull glanced at the sky. "Three o'clock white man time."

"Then we have to hurry." Annie said.

"I have been thinking," Cat said. "To do what you want to do, you must ask Tin and the monster."

"I thought the monster was just a monster," Annie said.

"True, but you need them."

"Even if we do," Hickok said. "Tin wouldn't be of any use. He's Doctor Momo's man."

"He loves the monster," Cat said.

"Say what?" Hickok said.

"Men," said Annie, "they are so dumb. I realized that the day Tin saw the monster lying on the beach. I thought he was going to melt."

"But…they are both…men," Hickok said.

"For one who thinks of himself as worldly," Annie said, "you know very little about love. Some men love men. And in a physical way."

"Well, I mean…yes, I've heard of it. I know it exists. But where do they put…it."

128

"Think about it," Annie said.

"But that is just wrong," Hickok said.

"Once you thought it was okay to kill Indians merely because they were Indians," Annie said. "Now you think that is wrong."

"That right," Bull said. "What about that, Wild Bill?" Then to Annie: "But me wonder too. Where thing go?"

Cat and Annie looked at one another, exasperated. "We'll explain it to you later," Annie said.

They went into the tunnel, flipped the switch for light, latched the door back in place, rushed along the corridor.

AT THIS SAME MOMENT, Doctor Momo, the quick-scooting Ned, and Jack—who was carrying Cody's babbling, smoking head on a platter as if it were that of John the Baptist about to be presented to the wife of Herod—were proceeding back to the living quarters of the compound.

THE EXPLORERS HAD NO SOONER pulled the rug in place, eased out of Doctor Momo's door and locked it, than they heard Cody running on about this and that, reciting some tall windy he had told them all twenty times before, but in a manner that indicated he was out of his head. Which, considering the circumstances, wasn't something he could spare.

Hickok and his crew hustled quickly down the hall, just out of sight as Doctor Momo, Jack, and Cody, turned the corner.

They all ducked into Bull's room, quietly locked the door.

Cat said, "I can only stay a moment. It is time for me to bring the doctor his tea. He gets upset if I do not bring it on time. But, I want to leave this key with you. Bull has one. You must be very careful."

"Thanks," Annie said.

They eased the door open. Cat glanced down the hall. "I must go," she said. She kissed Bull quickly and made her exit, leaving in the room the faint smell of musk.

Bull made a horse whinny under his breath.

DOCTOR MOMO STOPPED OFF IN HIS ROOM for a drink. He placed Cody's head on the table while he sipped whiskey. This time he did not offer Cody a drink. He stared down at the Westerner, shook the colored liquid in his glass.

Cody's hair was dripping sweat. His skin was less pink now, but it had a kind of glow to it. Cody felt great. He could feel himself changing.

The twisting knot on his neck had expanded, producing a large segment of shoulder. Underneath the shoulder, tendons were visible, and there was a spot of bone; blood dripped onto the metal tray, filled it.

Cody was about to ask for a taste of whiskey, when Doctor Momo spoke. "Drain that tray, will you, Jack?"

Jack bent over, began lapping blood from the tray.

"Good boy," Doctor Momo said. Then: "Colonel Cody, we have come to what I must call the moment of truth. Before this day ends you will have a shoulder, and perhaps a complete arm. A little luck, a hand and fingers. No more. There is hardly enough flesh and elixir left to provide more for you. I can brew up a bit of the beasts around here, make you part of them. But the ideal situation is a volunteer."

"Volunteer?" Cody asked.

"One of your mates. You need human flesh. I have offered up some of my own. And, might I add, without any selfishness. But, to do this right, to give you a complete body, and for it to be entirely human, we need a subject."

"You mean a flesh donor?" Cody asked.

"Of course. There's one little problem. I would really like to have someone not only donate a bit of flesh, but, in fact, donate their entire self."

"You mean kill one of them?"

"I dislike that word. Kill. It brings all sorts of nasty things to mind. Sacrifice is not a good word either. I suppose we could ask their permission, but, I am afraid, no matter how well they hold you in high esteem, donating their body to you might not be what they had in mind."

"I can understand a hold up on that," Cody said.

"But we are in a position, if we choose, to pick someone. We invite them to a special meeting, promise them something. Then we clip that sonofabitch in the head, and into the mixture they go."

"My God, Momo. I couldn't do that. They're my friends."

"Hey, your choice," Doctor Momo said. "You can be a head, a shoulder, an arm, and maybe a hand. But I wouldn't bet on much else. Or, we can choose one of the monkeys. You will most likely turn out a little hairy and have a craving for bananas and a desire to throw shit. I tell you what. I am going to have you taken to your room. Ned here will be left to serve you, and you may consider our discussion. But tomorrow, I would like an answer. I would like to pop someone before breakfast. Because, you see, Colonel Cody. I have other plans. I would like to do more with this flesh than reanimate you. I can build all manner of things from humans and animals. I can make you your very own Catherine. Would you like that? I can give you a body. A woman. If you go along with me, not only will you have your body back, but you and I can return to civilization, touting my work, and the both of us will become not only wealthy, but famous. I see myself as taking to cowboy hats, actually."

"I am already famous. And I am sometimes wealthy. When I don't waste it."

"Of course," Doctor Momo said. "I understand. And I am asking you to do a dreadful thing, no doubt. But, you either want your body back, or you do not. It really is that simple."

"My God," Cody said. "Think what you are asking. Civilization will not be glad to know we murdered humans for their flesh. And I won't be glad of it either."

"We do not have to tell the exact truth. Accidents happen. People die. There are ways around it. But, do not give me your answer immediately. To your room to rest. And to wait and see what my little experiment does. You may find yourself quite happy with the results. Jack. That is quite enough. Quit licking. The tray is shiny."

There was a light knock on the door.

"Ah," Doctor Momo said. "That will be Cat with my tea. Jack, will you see Colonel Cody to his room. And Ned, watch after him. And Colonel, give some real thought to picking out one of your little friends. If you do not pick one, I will pick one. And later, I will pick another. And when they are all gone— though I may keep Miss Oakley around for other reasons— Captain Bemo will bring me more. It will happen one way or another. The difference is, if I pick, you do not profit. In fact, I am sure you have considered this, but your head is flesh. And I don't believe in waste. A few slices, and you would fit nicely into the mixing bowl. Give it some thought, will you?"

As the day settled, well before dinner, Bull slipped out of Hickok's and Annie's room, returned to his own. Annie and Hickok decided to take a flyer. They crept out of their room with the key Cat had provided, moved along the corridor and tapped slightly on the door Cat said was Tin's room.

Tin opened the door, shocked to see them.

"We are friends of the monster," Hickok said.

"Bert," Tin said.

"Bert?" Hickok said.

Tin stuck his head out, looked in both directions, hustled them inside.

Bert lay on the bed nude. He was not the least bit embarrassed. Annie took him in with one quick look, then glanced away.

Then she glanced back.

Then away.

Then back.

And away.

"For heaven's sake, cover yourself," Hickok said.

"Heaven," Bert said, "has not been all that kind to me. I see no need to do anything for heaven's sake. Has your lady not seen a naked man before?"

"Do not tempt fate," Hickok said.

"I thought you were friends?" Tin said.

"I suppose we are," Bert said. "He and his friends saved me from being ground to powder. They carried me away and later

132

found me here on the beach. They saved me again. I suppose I at least owe the lady some respect."

Bert rose from the bed, snatched the sheet off and wrapped himself in it. "You may look now, lady, and forgive my manners. I have become quite the card as of late."

"Tin," said Hickok. "Will you help us?"

Tin said, "Help you? I should turn you in."

"But will you help us?" Annie asked.

Tin looked a question at Bert.

Bert said, "We could listen."

Hickok explained simply that they wanted to leave the island, that the best method might be by Bemo's submarine.

Tin said, "I will help you. I love Bert. I want to be with him."

"And I with you, Tin," Bert said.

"That is so sweet," Annie said.

"The problem we have," Hickok said, "is we have no weapons. We don't know how to navigate the Naughty Lass, and Bemo, who of course does know how, can't help us. He's controlled by Momo. What do we do?"

"Ned." Tin said. "He can operate the Naughty Lass."

"That's what we heard," Hickok said.

"I don't see why we don't just grab Momo and make him do what we want." Annie said.

"Because the monkey men protect him," Tin said. "They would tear you to shreds."

"We could threaten to kill Momo if they bother us," Annie said.

"They would still tear you to shreds," Tin said. "You might kill Momo, but they would kill you…oh, goodness gracious. How can I talk like this? Doctor Momo has been good to me."

"He has also lied to you," Bert said. "That heart business, remember."

"I remember. I am just so confused."

"We get out of this," Bert said, "we can go somewhere where we will not be bothered. Somewhere where we can live a life together."

"And where would that be?" Tin said.

"Maybe Annie and I can come up with something," Hickok heard himself say, and was amazed at the sound of his own voice. Just what was he thinking? He and Annie, a Tin Man and a monster who were sissy on each other.

"Another thing about the monkey men," Tin said. "You will not even get close to Doctor Momo. They seem to be out of sight a lot of the time, but they are near. They wait until he commands, or for that matter, looks in distress. When we eat dinner, behind the wall, to the right of Momo's seat. That wall is transparent from the opposite side. A kind of mirror. Monkey men wait there."

"Can we get guns?" Hickok asked.

"There are guns," Tin said. "I had not thought of that. We can get guns, but it will not be easy. There is a storehouse for such things. It is for the monkey men. Mostly it houses weapons they do not know how to use. Weapons the men who worked for Momo left. He sent them all away when he created the monkey men. He wanted complete obedience. The monkeys are less scheming than men."

"What about this storehouse?" Hickok asked.

"Guarded by the monkey men. But I can get in."

"Do you think Ned will operate the Naughty Lass?" Annie asked.

"He loves your Buffalo Bill Cody," Tin said. "I think he might. But then again, only if Cody wants to leave."

"And why would he not?" Hickok said.

"The body," Annie said. "You know that."

"And I know when the chips are down, Cody does the right thing."

WHILE NED SAT IN A CHAIR IN THE CORNER, curled up with a dime novel Buntline had written, titled, *Buffalo Bill Battles the Steam Dogs of the Prairie*, Cody lifted his new shoulder, flexed his arm, closed his hand and wiggled the two fingers and thumb he now had. It felt good, looked like his old arm, only stronger; in fact, he felt so vibrant he thought he might somehow be intoxicated from the chemicals used in the operation.

He was trying to consider who to offer Doctor Momo. Annie was out. She was just too sweet.

And Hickok. They had been friends a long time. He did not really want to have him boiled up and made into goo.

Bull. Bull was also a friend. But he was an Indian. Cody considered that he had certainly killed a lot of Indians in his time. Maybe one more wouldn't matter. Maybe that was the way to go. Just add to the record. On some level, Bull would understand that. He was a practical man.

Then again, would Indian flesh work with his flesh? Did that matter?

Cody let that run through his head for a while.

Bull became his favorite candidate.

IN HIS COFFIN IN THE JUNGLE, under three feet of dirt and leaf mold, Vlad Tepes, Dracul, could not sleep.

He hated that kind of thing. You needed to sleep. Wanted to sleep, and just could not.

It was terrible.

He had only recently started to have trouble.

Used to be, he laid down, his head hit the cushion in the coffin, and he was out like a dead man.

Oh, that was good. Dead man. He wished he had someone to share stuff like that with.

But...that was out.

Instead he was here with these creatures. They were not even proper men. They were made from this and made from that, and if the boar man he had tasted was any indication, they were a lot like the British. Bland. He had always preferred ethnics while in Britain. An Indian. A Chinese. They had some taste.

Their taste caused him to consider Asia in the first place.

Oh, the Americans had been all right, in spite of the smell. But they gave him indigestion.

Sometimes, no matter what you did, you just could not win.

Dracul closed his eyes and counted backwards from a thousand.

…eight hundred and seventy-one…Oh, this is not working. Not in any kind of way is it working. Eight hundred and seventy. Eight hundred and sixty-nine…

When he got to seven hundred and seventy-nine he lost count because he fell asleep.

The sun slowly sank toward the ocean. It was so red it appeared to be heated. The beast men gathered at the edge of the woods to watch it go down.

It made them nervous.

They knew they had to dig up their master when it was low down and the dark was high.

They knew they had to do that, and they would, but they feared doing it, and it was not just because Vlad Tepes, Dracul was ill tempered. It was something else. Something they sensed and could not explain.

The Lion Man said, "I know. Why don't we just dig him up now and eat him."

This was considered, and agreed to be a good idea.

VLAD HEARD THE GROUND BEING SCRAPED AWAY.

He sent out a telepathic message. *NOT YET, YOU FOOLS.*

The digging stopped.

Then it resumed.

I SAID STOP.

A pause.

The digging started up again. Now Vlad could hear them scratching on the lid of the coffin.

Oh, boy, was he going to whip some ass if they pulled off that lid.

The lid creaked, groaned, was lifted.

Beast faces looked down on him. Directly above his own face was the face of Wolf, formerly the Sayer of the Law.

The red rays of the dying sun fell inside the box and burned Vlad. He quivered, smoked, but could not make himself rise. The sun owned him.

I CANNOT STAND THE SUN. I MUST NOT HAVE SUN. REPLACE THE LID. NOW!

Wolf heard the voice in his head, and he wanted to do as he was told because he was afraid, but he wanted not to do what he was told because he was a beast and he was no longer a man and he did not have to listen to men, even one as powerful as this one.

"You ate Boar," Wolf said. "Bad man."

"Bad man," the beasts said together.

Vlad was cooking now, screaming, folding up inside his clothes.

But before he dissolved entirely, the beasts, in a frenzy, feasted on him, eating the smoking flesh quickly and finding it good.

If a bit bony.

TWO HOURS LATER, dark, the beasts sat on the beach and watched the waves explode in the moonlight, crawl over the rocks like some kind of frothy parasite.

"The bad man tasted good," Lion Man said.

Wolf stood up. He was wearing Vlad's cloak. He ran around the beach on his hind legs so that the cloak was caught up by the wind and flapped behind him like wings. The red underside of it looked orange in the moonlight.

Lion Man, who was wearing Vlad's vest, and nothing else, stood up and scratched himself.

"Momo, and all those men, they can kiss my ass. I am through with them. I am a beast. I can run on all fours."

He sprang about on all fours, shouting:

"I am free. ARE WE NOT FREE?"

The other beasts joined in. "We are free! We are free!"

"We bend to no man!" screamed the Lion Man. "We can eat anything we want. We can eat anybody we want. We can eat Doctor Momo if we want."

Wolf bounded into their midst.

"Oooooh. I don't know about that. Is he not our father?"

"Is he not meat?" said the Lion Man. "Do we not eat meat?"

The Goat Man said, "I'm sticking with vegetables."

They howled at the great big moon. They danced on the beach. They made love to each other. They drank spoiled fruit juice. They had a big time.

Of course, the next morning they were mighty sick, two of the creatures had bleeding asses, and the Lion Man, high on fruit juice, had eaten one of the goats.

Cody was ecstatic about having a shoulder, arm, and a partial hand. But the ecstasy soon passed. He wanted more. He decided he hadn't really liked Bull all that much anyway.

Bull it was.

He worked the muscles in his jaw, turned on his rotor and looked at Ned, curled in a chair, using his flippers and thumbs to read the Buntline book.

Old Buntline, Cody thought. Always there for me. Except when he was drunk. Or asleep. Or chasing whores. Well, there for me the rest of the time. Turned my crank when I lost my body. Listened to my bullshit stories. Made up bullshit stories about me that made me rich.

They had done all manner of things together. Back when he had a body.

God, he thought. A body.

Cody missed Buntline, but he missed his body more.

Damn, he thought. Ned Buntline. Ned the seal. What a coincidence.

Ned finished the dime novel, closed it, lifted his head, saw Cody looking at him. He smiled his little seal teeth. His whiskers wiggled.

With furious movement he laid aside the novel, pushed his glasses on his nose, grabbed up his pad and pencil, began to write.

Scooting down from the chair, Ned eased over to where Cody was, lifted the pad to show what he had written: I ADMIRE YOU.

"Why thanks, lad. That is most kind of you. I think you are quite the little cutter, yourself."

Ned began writing again. He held up the results: IT IS YOUR CODE OF HONOR I MOST ADMIRE. I HAVE NEVER KNOWN ANYONE LIKE YOU. I READ WHAT YOU SAID ABOUT LOYALTY TO FRIENDS. I WANT TO BE LIKE THAT.

Cody developed a lump in his throat.

"Why yes, little friend. That is important."

Ned jerked the page off, wrote on another, held it up: I WILL LIVE BY YOUR CODE. DO RIGHT 'CAUSE IT IS RIGHT...YOU HAVE CHANGED MY LIFE.

"Good...how good. Well now, I think I should close my eyes and rest, Ned."

Ned writing again. He held up what he had written: OF COURSE, SLEEP WELL. YOU ARE MY HERO. AND I KNOW YOU HAVE ALREADY DECIDED TO PASS ON THE DOCTOR'S OFFER. I AM SO PROUD OF YOU.

"Very nice," Cody said. "Very nice."

Cody closed his eyes to feign sleep. Maybe he could talk to Momo about banging the little seal in the head. Something quick and from behind, so he never knew what hit him. Have Jack do it. Better yet, Tin. Tin could hit hard and he seemed methodical. Jack would enjoy it too much. Jack would probably eat Ned when he finished. Must make sure that doesn't happen, thought Cody. No eating Ned. Just a quick bang and it's over.

DURING DINNER JACK CHEWED a lot more of Doctor Momo's food than usual.

Bert joined them for dinner this time. He sat by Tin, but they did not show any obvious affection toward one another. Beneath the table, however, their feet touched, and a couple of times, for what seemed like no reason at all to the other diners, the bolt between Tin's legs rattled.

Hickok sat and thought about all the monkey men Cat told him were behind the see-through wall. Hickok looked and saw only solid wall. Amazing. Was it true? Could there really be monkey men on the far side of the wall watching them?

Considering all the things he had seen here on Doctor Momo's island, there seemed little reason to doubt it.

Captain Bemo said not a word during dinner. He drank heavily and his face was gloomy.

Doctor Momo noted this with enjoyment, said, "Bemo, look at it this way. There is no use worrying over your plight. You are alive. You would have been dead. As for the rest of your life, well, it is mine."

After dinner, Bert was assigned his own room. Doctor Momo thanked Tin for watching after him. Tin escorted Bert to his room, presumably as a prisoner, but he left Bert's door unlocked. Jack led Annie and Hickok to their room, locked the door.

Doctor Momo himself carried Cody back to his room, Ned following.

Four armed monkey men helped the intoxicated Bull to his room. Bull had his arms around a couple of them, and was telling them a story in the Sioux language. They put him in his room and locked the door. One of the monkey men bent over and looked through the keyhole.

Bull staggered to his bed, sat down, stooped his shoulders, then fell backwards on the bed and lay still.

When the monkey man's eye went away from the keyhole, Bull sat up on the edge of the bed, straightened and smiled, sober as a minister at a baptism.

INSIDE TIN'S ROOM, Tin packed a small bag. It included: Machine oil. Polishing rags. A toothbrush. Mint water for a mouth wash. He opened the compartment in his body and took out Dot's silver slippers. He put the slippers in the bag, then pushed the bag into the opening in his leg.

Packed.

IN THEIR ROOM, Hickok and Annie kissed. After kissing, they exercised their fingers. Stretched them, bent them this way and that. They always exercised their fingers before they did any kind of marksmanship.

Of course, they were usually sure of having guns.

BERT SAT IN A CHAIR and thought about the skating championships. Shit, he had lied to Tin. He had purposely kicked that goddamn Frankenstein in the mouth. He had gone back for just that purpose. He would have to tell Tin the truth.

Then again, why?

They loved each other. Wasn't that all that counted?

CAPTAIN BEMO LOOKED AT HIMSELF in the bathroom mirror. He looked the same, but knew he wasn't. He hadn't been the same in a long time, and he didn't like it. He would never be the same, and he didn't like that. Even the load he had just dropped felt different. He had no desire to fornicate any more. Food was a chore. When science, eating, fucking and shitting were no longer fun, what was there?

He got a smaller mirror, turned so he could look in it; he could see the back of his head in the main mirror.

The bulb pulsed a dull yellow.

He remembered long ago, building the Naughty Lass with his original crew. He remembered how the crew jumped to his every command. Now he was lucky if someone would pass the salt.

Not worth it anymore, he thought. Being Momo's zombie is not what I had in mind for my life.

Bemo laid the mirror down, selected from his shaving kit his straight razor, and without opening it, using the mirror again, he pinpointed the bulb in the back of his head. Reaching over his shoulder, he used the closed razor to tap the bulb.

It was sturdy. It took the hit.

He did it again, but this time like he meant it.

The bulb popped.

Before Bemo fell to the floor, truly dead, he had the sensation of being on board the Naughty Lass, diving down quick into deep dark waters.

IN DOCTOR MOMO'S ROOM Cat grabbed a few things and put them in a satchel. A razor for shaving her legs. She still had a lot of fur to contend with, even if it did make her look as if she had a wonderful head of hair. She even had a faint mustache, but she stayed on top of it. No reason for anyone to ever know. She packed a toothbrush and a container of baking soda. Baking soda was really good for the teeth.

Gave fresh breath, too. She packed two Dickens novels and a small bottle of flea killer. She also packed two dresses and no underwear.

As he adjusted Cody's head on a dresser top, Doctor Momo said, "Did you give it some thought? About who goes to the meat machine, I mean?"

"I did," Cody said.

"And?"

"You can take your flesh growing business, all your test tubes, and stuff them up your ass, if there's any room in there after Jack climbs in."

"I beg your pardon?" Doctor Momo said.

"Hell, boy," Cody said. "You heard me. I don't stutter."

Ned snickered.

Doctor Momo's mouth collapsed and sucked wind. "You ungrateful American peasant. I will have you ground up and mixed with monkey meat. I promise you. Ned, take this talking head to my laboratory. Now."

Ned, glasses on his nose, jerked up his pad and pencil, began to write.

"What are you doing?" Momo said to Ned. "I didn't ask you a question. I gave you an order."

Ned turned the tablet around so Momo could read it: Kiss my little black seal ass.

"Why you ungrateful, glorified fish."

Ned wrote quickly, held it up: Mammal. You should know that.

Doctor Momo reached in his pocket, pulled a flick blade knife, snapped it open.

"I will have you gutted, sliced, cooked, and put on crackers, you piece of sea lard."

Doctor Momo slashed at Ned.

Ned moved just in time. For a seal on land, he was pretty fast.

"Leave him alone, you coward!" Cody yelled.

Doctor Momo turned, swung his hand at Cody's head, knocking it and the container that held him flying.

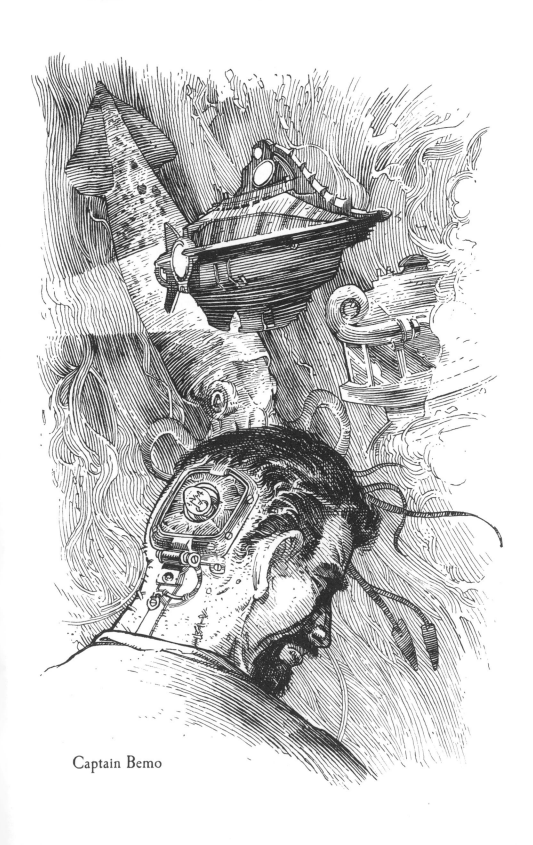

Captain Bemo

Cody rolled across the floor, slammed up against the door. Cody's new thumb popped back into his face and poked him in the eye.

"Owwwwwwww."

Doctor Momo turned his attention back to Ned, said, "Now where were we?"

Ned wrote quickly: YOU WERE TRYING TO CUT ME, YOU ASSWIPE.

TIN WALKED OUT TO THE WEAPON SHACK. There were two monkey men guarding it. They gave him a quizzical look. When he walked between them and took hold of the door, they began to chatter. One clutched his arm. Tin grabbed the monkey man's head and twisted it violently. It came off in his hands, messy and wet. He turned and threw it, striking the other guard full in the face. When the guard tried to get up, Tin stepped on his head. Tin was heavy. The monkey man was small. There was a sound like someone stepping on a pile of brittle sticks, followed very soon by a sound like someone stepping through a large pile of cow pies.

Tin shook the monkey man off his foot, grabbed the door to the shack once again, ripped it free. Inside was a virtual cornucopia of arms. Tin chose holstered revolvers, bandoleers of coordinating ammunition. He draped them over himself. He picked up a Gatling gun as if it were a pencil, as well as belts of ammunition. He tucked the Gatling under his arm. With his free arm, he scooped up a pile of rifles and shotguns, headed back to the compound.

On the way two monkey men approached Tin.

"What are you doing with that stuff?" one asked.

Tin tried to think of a quick answer. Nothing came to mind.

"Doc Momo said stuff was not to be touched unless he said so," the monkey man continued. "You are not doing some kind of bad thing, are you?"

"Well," Tin said. "Yes, I guess I am."

Tin kicked the inquiring monkey man in the testicles so hard the critter went out. The other one screeched, drew his revolver. But before he could fire, Tin dropped the Gatling, took hold of the monkey man's gun barrel, twisted it.

Next he twisted the monkey man.

When I'm oiled, he thought, I am one quick sonofabitch. He picked up the Gatling, kept going.

NED DUCKED DOCTOR MOMO'S SWIPE, rushed between the doctor's legs, knocking him down. In the process, Ned took a cut to his back.

Ned grabbed up Cody's jar, tucked it under a flipper, jerked the door open with his other, rushed out into the hall.

"Treason," yelled Doctor Momo. "Attempted murder. My seal has lost his mind. He's got Cody. Catch them!"

Monkey men appeared almost magically in the hall, sliding out of trap doors, slipping out of sliding walls. Ned saw them, but he didn't slow down, he went through them with his nose forward, his eyes half closed. He wasn't moving very fast, but he had some momentum. He knocked several of them over before a pile landed on top of him and hammered him to the ground.

WHEN BERT HEARD THE NOISE IN THE HALLWAY, he cracked open the door, saw the seal and Cody's head taking a beating. Monkey men were hammering the little seal, clanking on his tin head guard, kicking Cody's jar about. The jar slammed up against a wall and cracked, fell apart.

Cody stuck out a hand he had not had when Bert saw him last, grabbed the ankle of a monkey man and tripped him.

Bert rushed out into the hallway, grabbed a monkey man by the throat, squeezed until the throat went small. Then he grabbed up the dead monkey man by the ankle and went through the hall swinging the beast, knocking monkey men from wall to wall.

The monkey men went for their revolvers. The gunfire was loud in the hallway. Shots struck Bert. They hurt him, but they did not stop him. The monkey man he was swinging no longer had a head, just a red, wet stump. Bullets dove into Bert.

ANNIE AND HICKOK opened their door, saw the action.

Hickok burst out of the room, grabbed a revolver from one of the dead monkey men, started firing.

Bert and the Monkey Man

Every shot was a winner. Four monkey men fell dead. Then Hickok snapped the revolver on an empty chamber. The other cylinders were empty; the owner of the gun had already fired two shots at or into Bert.

Hickok grabbed up more revolvers, and now Annie was in the hallway, and she did the same. But by the time they did, a large number of the monkey men were dead by Bert's hand, and the others were fleeing so fast they were falling over one another.

Doctor Momo, who had been watching the action from down the hall through his partially opened door, closed it slightly and locked it.

Rushing to the wall behind his bed, he threw open a secret panel, hit the alarm button. He hit it twice. That was the signal for all the monkey men to congregate at his room.

ON THE OTHER SIDE OF THE COMPOUND, the alarm went off; a blaring horn, flashing lights placed strategically here and there.

The monkey men came together in a heap, chattering.

One of the monkey men, a survivor of the hallway fight, arrived with three of his comrades. He said, "That's the alarm. We all know what to do, but I think we might not want to. Big guy in there is wiping the floor with us. Ugly business. Monkey guts and brains from wall to wall. Bullets just piss him off."

"Doctor Momo calls," said one of the fresh recruits, "we're supposed to go."

"We been," said the first. "Didn't like it much."

"Doctor Momo needs help."

"You know," said the monkey man, unfastening his gun belt, letting it drop, taking off his shirt, scooting out of his pants, socks, and shoes, standing hairy in his underwear, "I've been thinking about eating fruit up in a tree. A lot."

"Me too," said another of the monkey men.

Others chimed in with the same sentiment.

Bending over, touching knuckles to the ground, they ran off into the jungle.

One diehard, still dressed as a human, said, "But what about Doctor Momo?"

"Fuck Doctor Momo," one of the monkey men called back.

The diehard stood for a moment, looked around the compound. He glanced hard in the direction of Doctor Momo. He glanced back at the open gate.

Beyond, the jungle, lush, full of fruit and grubs, beckoned him.

He slipped off his clothes, dropped to all fours, began to hoot and run for the jungle.

DOCTOR MOMO pressed the button again.

"All right now. Where are you simian sonofabitches? Things are not looking good here. Get your asses over here."

Jack pounded on the door. Doctor Momo looked through the peephole. He opened it, let Jack in.

"Where are those monkeys?"

"They stripped off and tore out for the jungle," Jack said. "They almost ran me down."

"Damn," Doctor Momo said. "What about Cat? Why is she not showing up?"

"I haven't seen her. But I did see Tin."

"Good."

"No, not good. He took a shot at me. He was carrying a bunch of guns under his arms, including a Gatling. He saw me and put them all down, took a rifle out of the batch and shot at me. I was lucky he was such a crummy shot."

"Why would he do that?"

"I think he's in with them, Doctor."

"Them? You mean Ned and Cody?"

"All of them. Hickok, the split tail, the whole lot."

"Bemo. We can escape in the submarine."

"No, that's not going to work."

"And why not?"

"Thought of that. Went by his room to get him, bring him here. He didn't answer the door, had to unlock it. He was on the bathroom floor. He popped his bulb. Was already starting to smell."

"All right. All right. If that's how they want it. They can

have it. We'll use the tunnel. Out on the beach, under a series of false boulders, I have a very fine boat. With a motor."

"A motor?"

"That's right, a motor. I built it with Bemo before I made you. You were a chimpanzee then. The boat is large, has a roof, plenty of room so we wouldn't have to share a bed, very fine equipment. It is well stocked. Dried foods. Water. Playing cards with nude women on them in compromising positions with farm animals."

"We could turn this into a holiday," Jack said.

"Just what I have always taught you, Jack. When life gives you lemons, make lemonade. Get the work books, my notes, and you and I will haul out of here. I will set the device to blow up the compound. It will blast their asses all the way to the moon."

"What about Cat?"

"Been nice knowing her," Doctor Momo said.

AS THEY ENTERED THE TUNNEL the explosive device started to tick. It was designed to blast the island into a large series of swirling dust motes. It was programmed to go off in forty minutes.

It took twenty minutes to get to the other side of the island.

It would take two to three minutes to activate the boat.

Then they would be gone.

Plenty of time.

The minutes ticked off on the bomb's counter.

ONE...

Hearing a commotion at the compound, gunshots and such, the beast men out on the beach gathered in a huddle.

"Doctor Momo's got some action going," Lion Man said, pushing his vest open, clutching it on either side like a happy politician.

Wolf agreed. He was still wearing Vlad's cape, and he had come to think of it as a sign of authority. Once it was the law, now it was the cape. Either way, he was the big cheese among the beast men and he intended to keep it that way.

TWO

"I say we go over there and eat Doctor Momo," Lion Man said.

"I don't know," said a creature so mixed of animals it was hard to know what he was. He was called Patch by the others. "He is still Doctor Momo."

There was another goat man in the crowd, and he thought of something he might want to say, then hesitated. After last night, after his friend had been eaten, he thought it best if he sort of went along to get along. He faded back into the crowd, tried not to bleat. He thought happy thoughts.

"I say we eat everybody," Lion Man said.

THREE...

Patch, gathering his courage, said, "I didn't want to bring this up, but, I think I should. There's a time when it has to be said. I think if we are going to live together, and if we are going to eat meat, that is all right. But I think a certain some-one amongst us needs to learn to draw the line. And we can't eat everybody all in one day. Do that, all the food for you meat eaters will be gone."

"I don't know," Lion Man, said, "there are always lots of monkeys."

"Food must be handled carefully," Patch said. "There is no such thing as an endless supply."

"That's a point," Wolf said to the Lion Man. "And, eating Billy, come on. He thought you and he were friends."

Lion's head drooped. "I couldn't help myself."

"And," said the other goat man, finally finding courage, "not all of us eat meat. I just don't have the teeth for it."

"All right, all right," said Lion Man. "I agree. Not to eat friends, that is the law."

"That's good," Wolf said. "I will put that on our new list. Not to eat friends."

"But," Lion Man said, "I still think we should eat Doctor Momo, monkey men, and that little Jack guy. Some of the others."

"That sounds good," Wolf said. "Let's march over there right now and get to eating."

"We can dig holes and put what we don't eat in the holes," said a dog man. "It tastes better after it's been in the ground a while."

"That'll work," Wolf said. They started for the compound.

FOUR...

FIVE...

SIX...

The monkey men were surprised to meet the assorted beast men at the edge of the jungle. It was not a happy surprise. A real wholesale slaughter went on.

SEVEN...

Monkeys were torn and ripped, thrown this way and that. A few fled into the trees, but they were heavier than when they were monkeys. They weren't as agile. Tree limbs broke. Feet slipped. It was not a good day for the monkey men.

EIGHT...

When wet monkey parts were spread from one end of the jungle to the next, the beast men continued their march to the compound.

Meat could be buried later.

NINE...

Bert, Tin, Hickok, Annie, Catherine, Bull, and Ned, carrying Cody's head, all came together near the dock where Bemo's sub bobbed in the dark blue water.

They arrived just as the beast men were coming out of the forest.

TEN...

"We see you!" the Lion Man yelled.

In response, Hickok and the others looked up to see the creatures charging toward them. There must have been a hundred of them, foaming at the mouth, cussing, one wearing a cape, another a vest, some in remnants of clothes. They were growling, running on all fours.

ELEVEN...

Tin, who was still carrying the weapons, dropped everything, called out, "Grab something."

Tin himself grabbed the Gatling gun, pulled out the props, adjusted a belt of ammunition, told Bert, "Guide the belt. Feed me, baby."

Hickok and Annie snatched up rifles, poked revolvers in their pants. They shoved ammunition in their pockets. Hickok said, "Ned, can you get the submarine started?"

Ned nodded.

TWELVE...

"Take Cody on board, start it up."

Ned hustled Cody's head onboard the submarine. Free of the jar, Cody was idly waving his arm about. Ned plopped Cody on the sub's deck while he worked the hatch with his two thumbs and flippers. It was a pretty tough job, but finally he jerked the lid open.

He grabbed up Cody, ducked inside, left the lid open for the others.

The Gatling gun began to bark.

THIRTEEN...

Creatures dropped. Wolf got a hole shot in his cloak. The goat took one in the stomach. Patch got a leg blown off.

A few of the charging beasts got past the Gatling barrage. Hickok, Annie, and Bull blasted away, killing the creatures. Cat managed to shoot the ground twice, knock fruit out of a tree, and nearly deafen Bull, she fired so close to his ear.

"Be better off, shoot self with that," Bull said.

"That's mean," Cat said.

FOURTEEN...

The beasts were on the run now. They grabbed up their wounded and fled into the jungle.

A cheer went up from the defenders.

FIFTEEN...

Patch and the goat were dead before they had been carried twenty feet into the jungle. The creatures stopped, laid their comrades down and looked at them.

SIXTEEN...

"They were brave," Wolf said.

"They were," Lion Man said. "Let's eat them."

"No eating friends, that is the law," one yelled out.

"Hey," Lion Man said. "Did we say anything about dead friends?"

"Well, now," Wolf said, "that's a point. It's not in the law. So, I suggest we eat them later."

SEVENTEEN...

This seemed agreeable. Their bodies were once again picked up, and the beasts, fed up with the Gatling gun, fled for the other side of the island.

EIGHTEEN...

The zeppelinauts and their comrades climbed into the submarine with their bags and guns. Hickok closed the hatch and Ned took her out.

NINETEEN...

Doctor Momo and Jack reached the end of the tunnel and attempted to lift the trap.

It moved only slightly.

"My God," Doctor Momo said. "It's hung. Give it a push, Jack."

TWENTY...

Jack gave it a push. It would not budge at first, then it gave.

It gave because the Lion Man, who had stopped to rest, was no longer standing on it. He had felt the movement beneath his feet and had stepped off.

When the trap opened, and out came Jack and Doctor Momo, the Lion Man and all the other beasts he had created were waiting.

TWENTY-ONE...

Wolf, the leader, said, "Well, Doctor Momo. What a pleasant surprise. For us, anyway."

"Welcome to dinner," said the Lion Man.

TWENTY-TWO...

"Just who do you think you're speaking to?" Doctor Momo said.

"Why, to you," said the Lion Man, reaching out to place a hand on Doctor Momo's shoulder.

Doctor Momo slapped the hand off. "I am your father. I am your creator. You will show respect. Sayer of the Law. What is the Law?"

TWENTY-THREE...

"I don't do that anymore," said Wolf, the Sayer.

"The hell you do not," said Doctor Momo. "Say the goddamn Law."

Wolf was surprised to hear himself say: "Not to run on all fours..."

The others began to quote it with him.

Jack grinned from ear to ear.

TWENTY-FOUR...

The Lion Man let out a bellow. "Stop! This is not our law. This is his law for us. We aren't his servants. Let's eat him."

The beasts stopped quoting the law. They exchanged glances.

TWENTY-FIVE...

"Wait," said Doctor Momo. "I am your father. Without me you would not exist."

"Not exist as we are," said the Lion Man. "We were something before you made us this. We are that again. Animals. I eat meat, Doctor Father. I like meat. You are meat."

"NO! I am not to be eaten. But you must be satiated. I see that now. I was wrong to deny you."

Doctor Momo wheeled, extended his arm, jabbed a finger at Jack, said, "Take Jack."

Jack looked sharply at Doctor Momo.

TWENTY-SIX...

"Doctor," Jack said.

But it was too late. Momo still had a certain power of command, and he had offered the Lion Man what he wanted.

Meat.

TWENTY-SEVEN...

The Lion Man sprang on Jack. The meat eaters leapt, ripping. Jack screamed. Briefly.

The nonmeat eaters cowered at the back of the crowd.

While the frenzy went on, Doctor Momo slipped away from the huddle, slid through a clutch of trees, broke for the beach.

TWENTY-EIGHT...

The Naughty Lass was still on the surface, cruising for deep water.

TWENTY-NINE...

THIRTY...

The beasts ate in a fury. They tore off Jack's head. It bounced above the crowd, every hand and paw reaching up to poke it.

Soon they were kicking Jack's head about the clearing.

THIRTY-ONE...

THIRTY-TWO...

Doctor Momo reached a pile of black rocks on the beach. They were built up high. Odd. Unnatural looking.

Because they were.

He bent over, pulled at one of the rocks.

It snapped open. Under it was a lever.

THIRTY-THREE...

Doctor Momo pulled the lever.

The ground slid open. There was a short flight of stairs.

Doctor Momo went down. Inside, in a hangar, was a large, streamlined boat. It was designed and painted to look like a black shark. It bobbed up and down in a channel of water.

THIRTY-FOUR...

Doctor Momo opened a hatch, climbed inside, pulled the hatch cover closed. He sat behind a V-shaped steering device. In front of him was a large, slanted window. All there was to see was darkness.

THIRTY-FIVE...

Doctor Momo worked a switch on the control board.

In front of the boat the rocks split open and there was light and the ocean.

THIRTY-SIX...

"Sorry, Jack," Doctor Momo said aloud. "I can make another man, but there is only one Doctor Momo."

THIRTY-SEVEN...

Doctor Momo pushed a lever forward and the boat jumped like a porpoise. It leapt into the light, tore out across the water in a burst of foam.

THIRTY-EIGHT...

The beast men quit kicking Jack's head about. The Lion Man took it and started to gnaw on it. He said, "Hey, where's Doctor Momo?"

"Gone," said Wolf. "He outsmarted us again."

THIRTY-NINE...

"Let's get him," said the Lion Man.

But, of course, it was too late.

Jack's Demise

FORTY.

The island rumbled, seemed to grow in the middle. The ground rose up and split. Trees fell. The compound trembled.

Then the whole island blew.

It blew with one terrific rumble and a blast. It knocked dirt, trees, manmade structures, beast men, and every living thing on the island into a mix of churning dirt and whirling explosives.

The explosion made the sea ripple. It made the sky dark. It spat a cloud up high and white as fresh sperm. The cloud spread. It took the shape of a mushroom.

THE SEA SHOOK as if it were gelatin. Momo's craft wobbled violently, but stayed afloat. It was making hot time, burning miles and splitting water.

It was doing great.

Momo laughed out loud.

Then the boat hit the side of the still surfaced Naughty Lass and blew into a thousand pieces.

It didn't do Doctor Momo any good either.

He went all over.

A chunk of him slapped up against the side of the sub's conning tower, hung there, then slipped off slowly and glided down gently into the water.

The impact knocked a hole in the side of the submarine big enough to drive a boat through.

The Naughty Lass took on water and began to sink.

INSIDE, NED SCURRIED with Cody's head toward one of the exit portals. He stood on the ladder and held Cody by the hair with his teeth. His little flippers and thumbs worked at turning the wheel that opened the hatch to the surface.

It sprang open, and up and out Ned and Cody went.

BULL AND CAT CAME RUNNING down the corridor, saw the open hatch, water sloshing in through it.

Bull pushed Cat toward the ladder, up she went, and up he followed.

They leapt over the side.

Tin and Bert were trapped in the library. The water had flooded in and was already up to their chests. There were only moments left.

"We've got to swim for the main hatch," Bert said.

"Never make it," Tin said. "We'd swim, then the thing would sink and take us with it. There may be another way."

"What way?"

Tin reached down, opened the compartment in his leg, took out his goods, pulled out the silver slippers.

"Yes," Bert said. "You can escape."

"Don't be silly. We both can or neither of us can. And this just might work."

Tin pushed the shoes onto his feet. His toes poked through the tips, his feet pushed out the sides.

The water was almost to their chins.

"Hold me tight, Bert," Tin said.

Bert clutched him. "I love you," he said.

"And I you. If it works, there's no telling where we will end up. It could be worse."

Bert looked at the rushing water, felt the sub start to tilt.

"And it could be paradise," he said.

Tin clicked his heels.

Nothing.

"It's not working," Tin said.

"It's the water," Bert said. "You probably have to click them harder. Give it all you got."

Clinging to one another, Tin moved his feet close together as the Naughty Lass tilted. He snapped his heels together with every ounce of metal and clockwork power he possessed.

The sub went under spinning.

But Tin and Bert were gone.

Hickok and Annie, once on the submarine, feeling they were home free, found Bemo's cabin and fell in bed together. They just couldn't contain themselves. Blood and violence made them horny. They were making love when the bomb went off on the island. They thought it was in their heads.

162

They were laughing at the joy of the moment when Doctor Momo's boat hit the Naughty Lass.

The boat collided exactly where their cabin was, ripped through. They never knew what hit them.

They were cut in half in their bed by a slice of metal fragment from the boat.

FAR OUT AT SEA Ned swam gracefully.

He had flung Cody's head on his back, tying it around his neck with Cody's long hair.

He had not bothered to check on Cody. He didn't know the water had shorted out the battery and breathing device in Cody's neck. Unaware of this, Ned swam on and on with the shriveling head of his deceased hero nestled on his back.

Two hours later the sharks took him.

Exhausted as Ned was, there wasn't even a serious fight.

WHEN BULL AND CAT leapt from the sub, they were fortunate enough to clutch to a piece of Momo's wrecked boat. A long seat cushion made of wood and leather.

It supported them for a full day before falling apart.

That night, they took turns with one swimming, holding the other up. Daylight, they continued the same program.

The next night while Bull was swimming, holding the fitfully sleeping Cat, he looked up at the stars. They seemed to be the eyes of lost friends, looking down.

He thought of Cody, Hickok, and Annie. He was unaware of their fate, but assumed they were all dead. He thought little of Ned, Tin and Bert. He hardly knew them.

Cat slept so deeply, Bull swam long after he felt he could swim.

Next morning, as it was turning hot and the skin on his lips was peeling in strips, just when he considered it might be best to go under, Bull spotted something.

Men on horses.

They were coming across the water.

They rode slowly.

They clopped their horses right across the top of the water and the waves curled at their feet like greasy grass.

As they neared he saw they were the faces of warriors he knew.

Crazy Horse. He Dog. Spotted Calf and several others he did not know.

Crazy Horse was dressed for war. He wore a dead hawk fastened to the side of his head. His face was painted with black dots and lightning bolts. His great white horse was decorated with painted hand prints, red and black.

He Dog wore nothing.

"My brothers," said Bull in Sioux. "Why is it that you come here?"

"We come for you, my brother," said Crazy Horse.

"For me?"

"For you and your squaw."

"I would ask you what horse pussy feels like," He Dog said, patting his mare's side. "But I already know."

All the warriors laughed.

"Here," Crazy Horse said, and extended a hand.

Bull took it.

He was pulled onto the back of Crazy Horse's mount.

When Bull looked down, Catherine lay asleep in a field of blue waving grass. He Dog climbed down, picked her up, and lifted her onto his horse. Spotted Calf reached over and held her sleeping body upright while He Dog climbed up behind her and held her with one hand and held his bridle with the other.

"Do not ride too close," Sitting Bull said.

He Dog laughed.

The riders tugged at their reins. The horses lifted their heads and rose to the sky, their legs working the air.

When Bull looked back, there was only the sea.

"You're awake."

Bull sat up. He was nude with a sheet over him. A man wearing a heavy blue coat and watch cap, smoking a pipe, was looking at him.

164

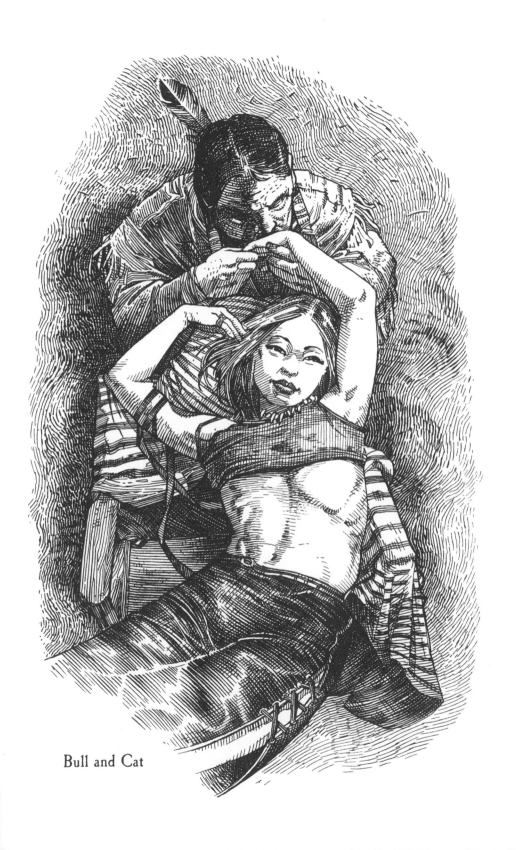

Bull and Cat

"Where am I?"

"On board a ship. We found you and the woman at sea. We sent out a smaller boat, pulled you inside, brought you here.

"So, did not die?"

"No," said the man.

"Woman?"

"She's all right. We have her in another cabin."

"No horses on water," Bull said.

"Excuse me?"

"Nothing. Bull thank you."

"That's all right…Are you the famous Sitting Bull?"

Bull nodded.

"I saw you in The Wild West Show once. You and Buffalo Bill. Just relax. You're on your way home now."

The man rose and went away. Bull lay back and pulled the sheet up under his chin. He closed his eyes. He dreamed briefly of the riders. Then he dreamed of Cat, and what they would do when they regained their strength.

The thought of it made him feel stronger already.

SOMEWHERE, IN A TIME OUT OF JOINT, there's an island and a beach. It's a better island than the island of Doctor Momo. It is full of trees and animals and the beaches are wide and made of pristine white sand.

Surrounding this beach is water more beautiful and a brighter turquoise than that of the Caribbean. The waters are full of fish. At night two moons race across the sky and the black between the stars is always filled with burning red comets.

The silver slippers hang from the limb of a tree bursting with fruit.

Tin and Bert live there.

Bert has fish and fruit to eat.

Tin uses oil made from plants and fish to keep himself functional.

All day they talk and walk and at night they lie together.

The sun comes up. The sun goes down.

The moons come up. The moons go down.

The Tin Man's chest feels warm, as if a heart beats there.

Bert, the monster Frankenstein built of dead bodies, feels very much alive.

And the two of them together, feel rich and full of soul.